Heirs to a Cause

A novel

Pascale Doxy

Heirs to a Cause

A Novel

Translated from French by Garry F. Doxy

Original publication : « *Les Enfants de la Cause* »
© 2023, Translated from French by Garry F. Doxy

Cover Picture:
Dionna Bright Photography
@2022, Pascale Doxy

ISBN: 978-0578-27798-1

Printed in the USA by Lulu Press, Inc.

To my mother…

Chapter 1

ith light touches, the elongated fingers of Anne Caroline Lebrun were diluting the pastel colors on the piece of paper. For the past hours, she has been trying to perfect this Hibiscus bouquet.

She took sand paper and sharpened the tip of her pastel pencil and meticulously traced the contour of a flower. She made a pause before wiping her fingers with a rag near a bowl filled with chocolate ice cream. Still concentrating on her drawing, she grabbed the bowl and finished the melting ice cream. Then she wiped her lips with the back of her left hand before lifting the paper. She tilted her head on one side and the other. She pushed away the paper to better examined the work. She liked the way the red of the petals was meeting the yellow of the pistils. She liked also the blue of the background sky – a deep blue like this last afternoon of summer school break.

Caroline showed a satisfied smile and stretched the length of her body. She stood up and moved away as she adjusted her shorts that were showing her long legs. At 17, she was taller than most girls of her age but she did feel to be an anomaly. She never bent her knees to reduce her height nor did her voice died in her throat in order to sound sweet. The world was hers to uncover, discover, and that is all she wanted to do. Completely lost in her own universe, she jumped a little bit when she realized her cousin was still standing in front of the dresser looking in the mirror.

On this Sunday, it was the umpteenth time she was watching Eva trying makeup and hair styles. She stared at her cousin for a moment. She did not understand her passion for cosmetics. The array of lip-gloss rivaled the rainbow and they were safely housed in casket. Then, there were her nail polish assortments. Eva, at times, even mixed colors to create new ones besides the ones she buys. It was only then that Caroline and Eva share an artistic sense. Caroline anticipated these moments to suggest some combinations or simply wait for the results.

Eva was a year older than Caroline and lived for her cosmetic *games.* And on this very Sunday afternoon, she was displaying all her fashion know-how. She straightened her hair, fixed it on the side, masked a blackhead, accessorized with the big loop creole earrings. Then, she delicately applied the lip-gloss for "important occasions"…

"It won't be a ball, you know," Caroline threw out at her.

"Tomorrow is the first day of class," returned Eva between two smacking of her lips. "You must make a good impression, my dear. You got to try this lip-gloss. The color fits perfectly your Mona-Lisa complexion."

Instead of a response, Caroline made a face. She grabbed a pillow on the bed and threw it at her cousin with all her might. Eva barely avoided the decorative pillow and it went crashing on the painting hanging on the wall. Carolina yelled in horror. She rushed toward the wall but gravity was faster. The frame fell at an angle on the white marble floor encased in golden acanthus leaf frame.

"Mom is going to kill me!" Caroline cried out.

The gaze of Eva's puzzled face half covered with foundation went from her cousin to the broken wooden frame.

"Why?" she asked confusingly.

"You don't know what this means to her!"

The painting depicted three women elegantly dressed. Though their faces were showing a sadness, they had an aristocratic smile on their lips. They stood straight in bouffant garbs finished with white gloves. Each woman was sporting simple dangling pearl earrings highlighted by the high hairdos. Caroline remembered that night when she first saw the painting – it was when her family moved to this Pacot neighborhood.

Built in 1946, the house was a mixture of traditional brick and modern Caribbean architecture. Continued renovations breathed new life into the home. However, that night it seemed too big, too old, too monstrous. Caroline's parents did all they could to lessen the blow of uprooting her from her childhood environment and school. The more they tried to explain, the more it felt as if everyone needed to be at the same place and time, in the same upper-class school. She visited every room until she settled in the present one. It was twice the size of her previous room with a bathroom and a large closet, almost the size of the room itself. The painting was hung on the off-white wall between two large windows. Right under, there was an envelope place over the floor.

"I am giving to you this little masterpiece that belonged to my grandmother. I know you will take care of it and you will defend its cause well. It belongs to you forever. Cherish and guard it tirelessly..."
-Tonton Blain

François-Ferdinand Blain was the original owner of the house and sold it to her parents. Caroline called this friend of her father's and grandfather's affectionately "Tonton Blain".

Being a bachelor, Tonton Blain adopted Caroline's family as his. He was a staple at their dinner table every Sunday. Caroline took in all the words and anecdotal stories he recounted from his childhood and globetrotting. But more than that, Tonton Blain was her ally in her unsatiable passion for the arts and antiquities. He knew also about of her desire to study abroad in the world's renowned artistic centers. Tonton Blain supported that desire by developing her aesthetic sensibilities. The painting was a token of that shared passion – a gift dated circa 1840.

Her parents showed some reticence because a thirteen-year-old girl, they said, could not possibly understand the value of such a gift. But François Blain insisted. He finally convinced Jacques and Micheline Lebrun that their daughter had talent to spare and that she had enough maturity to take care of the precious gift. Caroline did her best to merit this trust until this unfortunate fall…

Caroline took the painting and tried to fix the framing. Useless. The frame was made of wooden sticks that did not survive the fall. Time had already dried the glue that held the corners together. The young girl uttered a desperate sigh.

"Take off the frame. You can always say you didn't like it," suggested her cousin.

Eva Baptiste had a knack for finding good ideas. Caroline loved her more precisely in those moments. It has been a year since they have been sharing this room. Eva's parents emigrated to Canada and left her to the care of Caroline's parents until she could rejoin them. Caroline was happy to have a companion more adventurous than her. Eva took no time to integrate herself into the family and, at school, she gained everybody esteem.

Slowly, Caroline made a hole in the protective yellowed paper behind the painting. One by one, she took out the pieces of the frame that were sticking to it.

"What's this?" she asked perplexingly.

On the back of it, there was an envelope sticking to the sheet. Caroline's heart was pounding. In silence, she pulled out the envelope, opened it and read these written words:

"My very dear friend
Arrived have we in this country for so many years
Roaming about where nothing looks like ours, you can
Imagine our suffering for not being near you and able to
Elevate our cause.

-

Lest we stop searching, the distance between us
Or the sadness in our hearts will be the only
Unique way to deny our cause its denouement.
If you do not get discourage, you will find the
Second door through which you will
Enter victoriously… "- C.C.

Carolina's throat dried up. She looked at her cousin haggardly. She did not recognize the elegant, refined, nervous, and cursive hand writing. The letter was from a previous time, a time long past.

Chapter 2

aroline did not need an alarm to wake her up the following morning. In fact, she did sleep a wink the night before. She opened brightly her big eyes and was fixing the wall when the alarm sounded. She quickly smashed it with her outstretched arm. Her father's footsteps going downstairs made her jump. It was not often he was hurrying to court. That Monday was the day he would start to argue a new case in court. His assistant was already waiting for him at the Lebrun Law Firm. He decided to leave home early so that he would not be caught in the school traffic that was just starting.

The young girl turned her head and noticed near the pillow the mysterious letter. All night Caroline and Eva discussed unsuccessfully the meaning of the message. Carolina straightened up on the bed, read the letter again, and wondered: Where did it come from? Who wrote it? Are her parents aware of its existence? If so, why have they never talked about it before?

Caroline fell back on her bed. She stared at the adorned ceiling. A chandelier like that of her father's in the study was majestically hanging. The chandelier was an entanglement of golden acanthus leaves which the lamp glasses reflected. It was a beautiful decorative piece she admired and grew to love.

"This message is bizarre," she said finally. "Who is this C.C.?"

Eva already half-dressed started her morning ritual in front of the mirror.

"CC means Carbon Copy," she said while continuing to apply her make-up. "It must mean that someone else has the original of the letter."

Who could that be? Maybe Tonton Blain? What did he do with it? Why did he insist in giving her the painting? And why her?

The cause…Tirelessly…

These were the same words he wrote when he left the painting. She did not know of anyone suffering in a foreign country nor of researches to be done or a second step to take.

After much effort, Caroline got out of bed, stretched out a bit, and ran her fingers through her kinky hair. She carefully folded the letter and walked toward the closet.

"You're going to put it in your "casket of antiquities"?" Eva asked.

"Yes, while we understand what it all means."

Caroline appropriated an old suitcase of her father's and converted it into a trove of personal treasures. The "casket of antiquities", as her cousin called it, was fitting because all sorts of things that were hidden in there. Caroline had a collection of old stamps, copper jewelry which an elderly aunt on her mother's side left her, old family photos, and her genealogical tree in a notebook. Caroline slid the letter into the notebook.

A few shiny coins in a plastic bag attracted her attention. Tonton Blain gave her these coins when he was still alive. Caroline took one out and rubbed it against her pajama. On one side it read *Libertas Religio Mores HC 1808*. She flipped it on the other side.

"*Monnoie d'Haity 15 sols*," she said out loud.

"Why won't you make a bracelet out of them?" asked Eva over her shoulder.

"You're crazy! Put these century-old coins on my wrist as a bracelet! I would have my arm cut off!"

Eva looked up with desperation in her face while pulling her hair back. Caroline and her old things were amusing to her.

"Well to what use are they if you only keep them in the casket without ever showing them to anyone?"

Caroline smiled. Her cousin just gave her an excellent idea. As soon as she finds time, she would polish all the coins, put them in a glass picture frame, expose or hang them on the wall in the living room.

Caroline put back the coin in the bag and closed the casket. She wiggled her body and yawned. She still needed to wake up. In the shower, she closed her eyes and let the water run.

She was all awaken coming out. Her mind felt clear. She would need that clarity for the new school year, a year that would end with the national exam called *Baccalauréat*. She knew she would need that clarity also to solve this intriguing letter.

Carefully, she made her hair into a bun and tied it with a red and grey hairband that matches the color of her uniform. The bun highlighted her forehead and well-drawn natural eyebrows just above her deep brown eyes.

Caroline's mother was finishing her bread which was generously topped with peanut butter when she joined her in the dining room. It was rather a breakfast nook separated from the real dining room. The ceiling, like in the rest of the house, was high and every sound resounded in an interminable echo. It breathed the owners' passion for the arts. In the kitchen, in the TV room as well as in the living room there were chandeliers that gave the house a certain luxurious look. Among the paintings of Haitian masters that decorated the wall, the rock, iron and, wooden sculptors strewn about were a few of Caroline's watercolors. They could be seen even in the breakfast nook.

Caroline wrapped her arms around the neck of her mother who presented her cheek for a kiss. Her forehead and big eyes were the only things she inherited from her. Her mother was a petite woman with ebony skin and wavy hair. Caroline on the other hand was like her father, tall, slim with dark and kinky hair.

Caroline stopped a little in front of the large window above the sink. She liked the sprawling of the backyard. Between the Spanish lime tree, the Almond tree, and a few Cherry trees, she loved to rest under the pergola that occupied the middle of the yard just across a playing ground that her father constructed the summer before.

Caroline reached and grabbed a banana on the table.

"No, no," her mother protested with a soft and authoritarian voice. "Sit down and eat something that will hold you up. Quickly, please! We're leaving in twenty minutes."

Caroline pouted and dropped her bag on the ceramic floor. Summer vacation truly ended. Done the time where she could wake up late and eat anything she wanted for breakfast without her mother knowing because she had already left for the clinic.

Caroline went to the table and made an omelet sandwich. Leaning on the sink, she nibbled at her breakfast just as her cousin was entering. Eva's makeup was perfect. Her foundation was barely visible. Her long eyelashes were fanning under her perfectly plucked eyebrows. She was like a beauty contestant ready for her challengers.

Eva greeted her aunt before she sat at the table. They both shared the same features – same skin tone, wavy hair, and height; just the youthful voice of Eva broke the similarities.

"Five minutes!" yelled out Dr. Micheline Lebrun to her niece and daughter.

Eva reacted surprised by the statement of her aunt and Caroline smiled a little. Her cousin ate quickly as her aunt already stood up out of her chair.

Relentless beeps came from her mother's bag. The pager had a message. She took out the device and read out loud: "Dr. Lebrun stop at the maternity ward of the General Hospital this morning."

"Well, you heard the message," Dr Lebrun said while putting the pager back in her bag. "We have to hurry!"

Caroline looked at the small device. At least, she taught, her mother was keeping hers in her bag and was not showing it off like her father was doing. He had his hanging on the side of his pants. They were so close to the 21st century and Caroline wondered when would her parents finally decide to learn about cell phones.

"Girls, you have the number for our pagers, right?"

"We sure do," replied Eva.

"Good. By the way Caroline, your friend Natalie called last night to remind you to bring her CD today."

"She's crying for her CD while it's been two years since she lost my book," cried out Caroline.

"What book?" her mother asked while grabbing the car keys.

"The novel Tonton Blain gave me. She never returned it."

"Caroline, really! That's not something you lend to people. When will you understand how to take care of your things?"

Caroline did not answer. Her gaze met her cousin's. All of this for just a book. Only if her mother knew what happened to the painting, she would really loose it.

"Mom, it's just a novel...Natalie and I trade books all the time."

Her mother looked at her disapprovingly.

"*Tirelessly...* Tonton Blain for sure didn't have any children."

"What?"

"Only people without children would tell them to keep something *tirelessly*."

"But...," said Caroline completely puzzled, "when did he say that?"

While Caroline was speaking, her mother opens the car door to encourage her and her cousin to get in.

"He said it," replied her mother, "when he was giving it to you. You don't remember that? You responded, yes, though."

Of course, she remembered the novel. But to 'keep it tirelessly'? Was the novel hiding the second step?

"What else did he say, mom?"

"I don't remember anymore, Caro. I don't remember…"

Caroline read the novel once. She liked it enough to have talked to her friend about it and lent it to her. The story was interesting but she didn't remember any outstanding revelation that would link the novel to the letter. Now, she must insist that her friend returns it. To what mystery Tonton Blain was pushing her into?

Chapter 3

udubon School, a decades-long landmark, located in the center of the city, was a private school sat on a half block along with a mixture of businesses and private homes. It was not unusual to hear a constant beeping of horns voicing the impatience of drivers in the jammed traffic. The students, either on foot or in the interminable line of private cars, were threading, more or less quickly, toward the school.

A few street vendors were already setting up on the sidewalks. Among them. Caroline recognized one selling *fresko* (a shaved ice with various fruity syrups). Next to him, his ever-present wife selling roasted peanuts, little bags of *chanm-chanm* (a sweetened mixture of grinded peanuts and corn), and *tito* (candy canes with a taffy taste). They have seen generations of students while sitting on those sidewalks. Both cousins greeted them cordially before entering the gates of the school.

The school was spread over a large area. A big playground surrounded by stands served as a link between several buildings that housed students from different sections. They were whitewashed with lime. The front yard was crowded with high school students. The cries of joy rang out. Some students got together to show off their new bags, their fashionable shoes, their latest gadgets. Around them or under the almond trees, the newcomers clung to their bags, intimidated by so much excitement. A few students, accompanied by their parents, formed a line that went around the entrance and the school bookstore which were both located under the building of the high school section.

As soon as they entered Caroline and Eva separated to find their respective friends.

"Caroline!" shout out a voice from a group of students.

"Natalie!"

A young girl of average height with dark brownish hair and almond-eyes came and hugged Caroline.

"I thought you would never come back from vacation, Nat!"

"I just came back yesterday! Girl, do I have a few stories to tell you!"

"I have your CD," Caroline said abruptly. "You have my novel?"

"Wow! Relax…Yes…My little brother hid it under a pile of toys…There you are madam!"

"Finally!!!"

The novel looked worn out but Caroline did not notice that at first. She grabbed it and quickly put it in her bag.

"Oh, the schedule! We must see where we have our classes."

The lists of the high school classes were affixed on a cork board on the first floor. Since 4th grade, Caroline and Natalie were always in the same room. Yet, each year they feared a separation. As they made their way to the board, two other girls ran up to them and engaged in an endless exchange of kisses and hugs. A gathering of students was already and carefully examining the lists. One of the girls volunteered to check for the rest of the group. Except for Caroline and Natalie, all their friends were in separate classes. There were disappointments all around. Caroline and her friends faked sobbing and then burst out into laughing.

At 7:30 a.m. the school's bell rung, calming the heightened spirits. Students with signs guided the lines that needed to be formed. Caroline and Natalie went to the 11th grade A sign and stood in the middle of the line. Their eyes wandered everywhere to get an overview of the freshmen who were in other rows as well as the first hour teachers. Caroline's gaze met that of her cousin holding the sign for 12th grade.

After the raising of the flag, the principal, a woman in her fifties, addressed the assembled students with an impassioned, strong, and authoritarian voice. Caroline sighed. She knew that after addressing the middle school students, the principal will follow through with the 9th and 10th graders to finally give her longest speech to the seniors.

"For the younger ones, you seniors should be examples to follow. By your diligent work, seriousness, and involvement in the culture of the school, you will encourage the others to excel. Every year, our school is among the most successful at the national exams of the Board of Education. The teaching staff and myself know this year will not be different. You will make us proud…"

Caroline was barely paying attention to the principal's speech. She thought she recognized a familiar face in the crowd – one of Eva's friends. Finally, the assembly of students was dismissed and they silently walked to their classrooms.

The students in Caroline's class rushed to the seats they judged to be the best near the large windows. The front rows were left as undesirable. Caroline and her friend chose the left front seats closer to the wall. Their choice was strategic because little did the students knew that the ones close to the wall would shield them from the burning afternoon sun.

The first period teacher was already standing in front of the green blackboard and was writing the date with white chalk: Monday, October 5th 1998. As no one was paying attention, he finally turned around, and cleared his throat.

"Good morning," he said firmly.

All the students returned the greeting.

"I am Mr. Georges Alexandre, the history teacher for the year."

Natalie giggled.

"Yaks! Where did he get this get-up?"

It was obvious to all that their history teacher was a fashion disaster in need of rescue. He was wearing a washed brown jacket over a crème shirt with a worn-out multicolor tie. His hair did not take to the black coloring he intended and gave him or accentuated a premature greyish look. Though with such an appalling appearance, Caroline was captivated. From what Eva told her, who took the class the previous year, he was a teacher with great passion. She was glad to have taken the class. He made her appreciate the subject even more.

"I will be seeing you all once a week. You will have several research papers throughout the course of the year. If you have questions, please ask them BEFORE the due date. I am here to help."

There was a low rumbling in the class and a student behind Caroline raised her hand.

"Where are we going to do our research, sir?"

"Where ever you want. Just make sure your papers are typed or handwritten on folded papers...Don't worry. We'll get it done...Now, it is time for the presentations. Let's start with the back row."

The requirement of a recurring paper brought down the spirits of many in the class. Some had their heads down on their desks; some were bent backwards in their seats. A few students from the back were already presenting themselves, when Caroline straightened up abruptly.

"What is it?" asked Natalie.

"I know this voice. It's him."

"Who? You know him?"

"That's a friend of my cousin."

Natalie turned in the direction of the male voice. He was about 6 feet tall; he had a light muscular built with mischievous cinnamon-colored hair and eyes. He stood out from the class.

"You two yentas, please present yourselves," said Mr. Alexandre.

Caroline tensed up a bit. Two yentas? That was not the way she wanted that teacher to view her on a first day of class. She rose graciously from her seat presenting herself and added that she was very impatient to dig into the subject.

"Miss Lebrun, I am happy to hear that and the curriculum will be challenging. However, class as you know who wants…"

"Who wants June prepares in October." The class finished in unison.

"Very well," said the teacher with a little smile. "Please take your book and let's see a few highlight… Miss Lebrun would you please read for us the first three parts that we will cover this year?"

Caroline was happy that she might have corrected a bad impression the teacher might have had of them.

"Yes, Mr. Alexandre."

Natalie, however, was a little distracted by the young man in the back row. She was constantly turning her head to look at him.

"We will cover: The evolution of the Revolution of Saint-Domingue, Toussaint Louverture and the Revolution of Saint-Domingue, the War of Independence..."

"Very good, Miss Lebrun. Before we get into it, I would like to do a little mental exercise that will get the history juices flowing...Please form groups of 4. Students in front, you will turn to face the ones behind you."

The class reluctantly and slowly followed the directions. The moving of the desks created an instant cacophonous noise. If most of the students were somewhat happy to work with their friends, Caroline felt that she was not Natalie's first choice. Her friend's eyes were going straight to the back row.

"First," continued Mr. Alexandre, "I would like for each group to discuss what they know about the different colonization that Haiti and other Caribbean islands went through. Write them down in columns."

To help speed up the exercise, the teacher wrote on the board the theme 'Colonialism' and made two columns with heading 'Country' and 'Colonialization'. The students seemed to have changed their minds about the exercise and started to execute enthusiastically the directions now. The period went by fast. The school's bell rang for lunch. Natalie got up quickly and rushed to the back of the class.

Staying behind, Caroline was leafing through her novel. Facing the back to the class, she paid no attention to her surroundings until she heard a familiar voice.

"Caroline."

"Lu..." she said hesitantly while rapidly closing the novel.

"Ludovic," said quickly Natalie. "Ludovic Xavier Paul."

"I see you have already got really acquainted."

Ludovic gave out a furtive smile but ignored the remark. Caroline met him just once before during the summer vacations when her cousin was having a pizza party. The group of friends filled one entire section of the restaurant while their parents were on the other side.

"Have you already seen Eva?"

"Eva is in the school?"

"Yes. She's in *Philo*, the last senior class."

"If you want," suggested Natalie. "I can show you where is her classroom."

"Ok. See you later, Caroline."

Caroline watched Natalie and Ludovic walking away. "Here we go again!" she said to herself. Yes, Natalie was her friend but Caroline understood less and less why she always seems to find a new beau every year.

She was happy though that they left; she wanted to read the novel and maybe find in it something interesting. She read the description on the back cover – it was an impossible love story in 19th century England. The novel was in bad shape with greasy pages, some upturned corners, and even color crayon markings. This was no surprise; Natalie always did this with every novel. Caroline decided she had had enough of that and that it will be the last book she will ever lend her.

She continued examining the novel without any success. The title did not appear to have any significance. Then she opened the book and read:

> *March 14th, 1995*
> *Follow through Caroline.*
> *I hope you will love this second step.*
> *-Tonton Blain*

Caroline's heart jumped. Was that a clue? Could this second step be in the novel? The note on the back of the painting mentioned something similar.

She put the novel in her bag and quickly ran out of the class. She needed to talk to her cousin. She took to the stairs in haste barely running down some students sitting on the steps.

Groups of newly minted friends were forming on the school's yard. Caroline scanned impatiently the groups but could not spot her cousin. She went to the crowded cafeteria. An odor of French fries, ham sandwiches, *pâté*, and spaghetti permeated the room. A voice from the back of the cafeteria caught her attention; she went toward it.

"Where did you go?" Natalie asked.

"Hey, guys! I'm looking for my cousin. Have you seen her?"

"The last time I saw her," said a boy, "she was walking toward the dean office."

The smell of her friend's lunch made Caroline's stomach growled. She looked at her watch: she only had a few minutes left before the end of recess. The next break was at noon and she was not sure her stomach would hold on until then.

Chapter 4

aroline was distracted the whole day. After reading the novel's dedication, she could not concentrate on any school work. At the second break of the day, she could not meet her cousin at all because Eva was occupied in organizing the election of her class committee. When school ended, Caroline's mom was already in line to pick them up. She had no choice but to wait until she gets home to share with her cousin her new findings.

The ride back home was taking a long time. There was traffic jam everywhere. It was the rush hour and the heat was taxing humans and vehicles. Not all the traffic light were working throwing buses and private cars into a fight where only the most aggressive ones would win. Amid that struggle, the pedestrians were doing their best not to get hit while choosing to cross the street without any indication of what was the best time to do so.

An idling taxicab became disabled just in front of Dr. Lebrun's car. Smoke was billowing from the hood. The taxi driver defeatedly came out and the passengers angrily exited the vehicle.

"This can't be for real!" she yelled out while letting her head fall on the car's headrest.

The taxi driver tried to cool down the heated motor with a gallon of water and a few charitable souls helped him to push the vehicle on the side of the already crowded street. All of this added to the stress of the day for Dr. Lebrun and the impatience of Caroline grew by the minute.

"I am glad that your father will pick you both from now on in the afternoons. Because after a day in the clinic, I could not be stuck in this traffic every day."

Caroline said nothing still having her mind on the novel which she took out of her bag. She did not notice her mother's gaze.

"Natalie returned it to you."

"Yes, but in bad shape."

"Let me see," said Eva from the back sit.

"There's a dedication," said Caroline to her with her eyes wide opened.

Eva understood the hint and grabbed the novel. She silently read the dedication before going rapidly through it.

"Did you notice that, Caroline?" she cried out a few minutes later.

"Notice what?"

"There are some pages missing."

"You're kidding me!"

Besides being mishandled, the novel was also missing pages. What if these missing pages contain crucial information? Now, how is she going to understand the whole story? Anger and disbelief ran through out in Caroline's body.

They were finally home. Caroline's mother honked repeatedly to attract the servant attention so he can open the gate.

"We can always buy a new copy," she pointed out to her daughter.

"Yes, please. But I want to keep this old one."

Caroline's mother looked at her puzzlingly, unable to understand her daughter's passion for old things.

Out of the car, Caroline rushed to the kitchen. She only wanted a bottle of fresh water but the smell of white rice, slow cooked blue crabs with *lalo* vegetable and red beans puree tingled her nostrils. They came at the right time. The cook was just setting the table. Caroline cracked a crab's leg and put it quickly in her mouth.

"Go wash your hands, young lady!" Dr. Lebrun said.

Caroline wiped her hands on a napkin, gave a kiss to her mother, and rapidly climb the stairs to her bedroom.

Eva was already taking a shower. She did better in resisting the delicious food. Caroline walked to her desk and dropped her bag. Before taking the novel out of her bag, she opens the napkin on her desk and put the crab legs on it. She opened the book to read the inscription one more time. It gained now a lot more importance for her. She could have never imagined that Tonton Blain was hiding something.

Eva came out refreshed.

"Did you see the Inscription?" asked Caroline while unlacing her shoes.

"Yes."

"To think about it, the novel must be the second step."

"That's what I think too."

Caroline thought that after dinner, she could read the entire novel again. But she had a lot of homework and it was a thick book.

"What if we divide the book in sections?" she said to her cousin. "I would read the first twelve chapters and you the next twelve."

"What about the missing pages? I think we should wait for the new copy. We would be sure to miss nothing."

"Yes. But with two copies, it would be better. We would go faster too."

Eva walked to her bed, took a notebook out of her bag before grabbing from her night stand an address book. Carefully, she transcribed all the names and their phone numbers from her notebook to her address book. Caroline was amazed at her cousin social skills. She could not believe that in one day she made so many friends.

"*Redingote* and all the other teachers loaded us with work," Eva sighed.

"Mr. Alexandre is so nice. I don't see why you guys gave him that name?"

"You'll see why soon. It'll be a real fashion runway of poor taste!"

The room was getting hotter with the penetrating sunrays despite the fan running at full speed.

"Ludovic is in your class," said Eva.

"Yeah...You saw him?"

"You'll like him. He's cool... Girls are dying for him."

Caroline already witnessed his effect on them. Natalie's showed a jealous face when she learned that Ludovic was not only a friend of her cousin but also one of her neighbors.

"He's an artist like you. You should see his drawings. That guy is a genius! I think I have one of his drawings somewhere."

It was the year before, at a concert that Eva met Ludovic. The entire city was awaiting this very popular American band. The cameras of MTV were broadcasting live this once in a lifetime concert. Caroline's desire to attend was met with her parents' resistance. Finally, after many discussions, they softened their stance knowing that Caroline and her cousin would be with a group of friends they knew. Unfortunately, Caroline got sick that day and missed the breathtaking sunset behind the stage near the ocean at the *Bicentenaire* boardwalk and the unforgettable memory-making fun she would have had to sing out loud the chart busting songs of the group with her friends.

"Look!" said Eva who was showing the drawing to her cousin.

"Wow! He's really good!"

"I told you," Eva replied before going downstairs to the kitchen.

On a gray piece of paper, a life-like fusain drawing of Eva testified to the talent of Ludovic. The interplay of dark and light charcoal strokes was made with ease and dexterity. The copy was true to the real subject in more ways than one.

Caroline was staring at her works on the wall. None were comparable to Ludovic's.

Her father's voice took her out of her contemplation. He was standing in the door frame in a navy suit. His yellow tie was loose. A folder in one hand, he was handing a calculator to her.

"I'm giving you mine," he said in his deep voice. "Tomorrow when I pick you up, I'll buy you a new one."

"Thank you, dad…I will also need a book."

"Your mother told me."

Mr. Lebrun touched his daughter's chin before inquiring about her first day at school. While talking to her father, Caroline was still holding Eva's portrait.

"Wonderful drawing," noticed her father.

"Eva's friend did it…Maybe one day, if I have the chance to study art, I could draw as good as this."

Mr. Lebrun smiled a little and looked at his daughter ever so kindly.

"We talked about it many times, Caro. You will be able to study art as soon as you finish Law school. You can combine both actually and be an intellectual property attorney."

Caroline gave out a little sigh. She knew she will not win this one. Between an attorney father and a pediatrician mother, she often felt boxed in. How can they not understand that the white physician blouse is not her favorite fashion or the sound of the gavel in a packed courtroom not her favorite music? She wanted to create, invent, give free reign to her imagination and the wildest ideas.

"I want to just study art."

"Do you know Charles?" her father asked. "He's an art expert that we use all the time. He's been working with us for years. Imagine you will have that expertise yourself and you can grow the practice even further."

Mr. Charles Philippe, another art fanatic that Caroline could have also called "Tonton" if he was not constantly giving her the impression that he was chasing after something. The auctioneer was always in hurry and Caroline had the impression that she only caught a glimpse of him every time she met him. It had been a few years since Tonton Blain introduced him to her family. Like many of the old man's friends, after a career abroad, he decided to return home to live out his retirement. But the auctioneer soon got bored and offered his expertise to the Lebrun Law Firm.

Caroline sighed. Her face was a sad contrast to her determined father's. His dream was to see Caroline take over the law firm that his own father passed on to him.

"Come on, young lady! It's time to eat. Everybody is already downstairs."

Caroline gently dodged her father's hand as he was about to touch her hair. She almost forgot she was hungry. She put down the drawing on Eva's bed, picked up the novel, and went down to the dining room.

Chapter 5

espite the missing pages, Caroline did not lose interest in reading the novel. When her father took her to the bookstore the next day to buy a new copy, she had already read the first three chapters of the worn book. To her relief, most of the damaged pages were at the end and nothing was amiss. However, despite her determination the school year was starting to take a toll on her.

Eva seemed to have time for everything while Caroline struggled under the load of home works and assignments. Eva took up a new hobby: tennis. She spent hours playing with Caroline's father. Once-and-while, Ludovic was invited which made the games animated and more competitive. Caroline's mother always blamed her rheumatism and was content to be, depending on the day, a cheerleader for her husband's or her daughter's team.

One Saturday where the players decided to seek other activities and interests, Caroline joined her mother under the pergola wanting to read the 12th chapter of the novel. Soon her father took a seat. The rain from the previous day was forcing the temperature to get cooler and the almond tree was losing its leaves. Not too far from her aunt rocking chair, Eva spread her collection of nail polish and was retouching so gently her nails with one of her inventions.

"Eva, can I try that red when you finish?" said Dr. Lebrun

"Okay, auntie. I can put it on for you, if you want?"

Caroline finished the chapter and did not notice anything of interest in her reading. She laid lazily pensive on her chair and a bit disappointed. She passed the book to Eva who understood that it was her time to read.

Caroline stretched out her limbs and reached for her sketchbook. Ludovic also had one. Since she saw his, she taught it was a better idea than drawing everywhere on her notebook or simply on a piece of paper. Her friend's drawings renewed her desire of becoming a great artist and she decided to draw every day.

Caroline flipped through the previous pages. This sketch book was her fifth. It was the one intended for the study of the human body. That afternoon, then, the center of interest was her toes. Caroline lifted one foot and looked at her short-cut nails. They had never worn such a fiery red polish as the one her mother had chosen.

"You finished the science homework?" asked suddenly her father.

"I think…"

"We must find you a tutor for these subjects," her mother added. "They're very important parts of the Bac exam."

Caroline tilted her back a bit to look at the sky. The little time she had left is now going to be taken by tutoring.

"I'll be ok, mum. There are kids in my class I can work with."

"We'll see," her father said. "If by December your grades haven't improved, we'll get you a tutor…And you Eva, you have nothing to do?"

"I just finished writing an essay on farming issues between the years 1804 and 1843…Redingote is horrible! It took me eight days to write that essay!"

"Redingote?" Dr. Lebrun asked.

"That's the name the kids gave the History teacher," Caroline answered. "He always wears colorful weird-looking jackets. But I really love his class."

"I prefer Sciences and Math. They're practical, tangible," Eva said.

"I find Social Studies and Languages to be more interesting," Caroline argued.

Caroline's father took a sip of coffee before setting his cup down on a small iron table beside him. He crossed his two hands behind his head, stretched his long legs forward.

"Ah, I remember... Man! History was my favorite subject, especially in my senior year. My teacher's name was Mr. Paul.... By the way, girls, I found out that he was Ludovic's grandfather," Mr. Lebrun said.

"Really!" replied Caroline.

"Yeah... This man was a scholar! He was an abyss of knowledge... I hope Ludovic is as intelligent as him."

Caroline could not give her opinion on that. In class Ludovic was always quiet. He did not participate in discussion and answered a question only when he was directly asked. Despite of that, his affable smile and pleasant eyes attracted everyone, especially the girls.

"Tonton Blain was Mr. Paul's brother. And just like him, he was also a lawyer."

"Why didn't he have the same last name?" questioned Caroline.

"At the time the birth certificate was being generated, they switch the first name of the father for the last name."

"How could that be?" asked Eva.

"Sadly, some provincial officers don't take care in verifying neither the spelling nor the true names of the constituents. I had to represent several families when disputes arise in relations with heritance and things like that. An attorney must use innovative research technics. Anyway, I was the one who represented Tonton Blain in his court case against his brother."

"Your father was so distressed during that time!" added Dr. Lebrun.

"It's never easy to be in the middle of a family dispute, especially if it involves friends."

Mr. Lebrun ran his hand over his freshly cut hair. The embarrassment he had felt during that time was still visible on his face.

"It's after this that Tonton Blain put his house for sale."

"But why?" asked Caroline.

"I think it was the realization that he was alone with no genuine family in this big house. Added to that, he was severely ill."

Caroline remembered that day that Tonton Blain revealed his terminal cancer. Back then, she was too young to understand the full effect of that news and the severity of the illness. She thought a doctor or even her mother could prescribe some medicine and that would be the cure like a cold. Patiently, her mother found the words to explain his march toward death. She cried all night the inevitable end of this dear confident.

"I'm still baffled by the way we were offered the house," added Dr. Lebrun

"Why do you say that auntie?"

"Your auntie and I didn't have all the funds to buy it outright. We did so by installments."

"I wondered if it was a way for him to assure his living expenses," wondered Dr. Lebrun.

"I would say instead upkeep expenses for the property…There were always some renovations going on," said Mr. Lebrun.

At first, Caroline did not like moving into this new house. But the architecture, the finishing, especially the flooring in her room and her father's study won her over. The design of the marble floors and the delicate molding encasing a grandiose chandelier were hidden gems in the overall architectural charm of the house.

"I have the impression that he loved your office the most, uncle."

"Yes. It was his favorite room."

"You know, I think that he probably didn't want his brother to inherit the house," pointed out Dr. Lebrun.

"Maybe that was why he was constantly telling me that he was doing so in order for God to help him defend his cause."

Caroline and Eva exchanged a puzzling look at once. The phrase flashed in their minds like a lightning bolt.

"Do you know what he meant, dad?"

"He never actually explained what he meant. I just assumed that the illness was taking a toll on him, with the stress and all. At one point, *To defend the cause* became a sort of moto for him."

"Honey, do you remember when he gave you that small painting in the living room?" ask Caroline's mother to her husband.

The small painting was a tropical landscape that Caroline always has seen at her house. It had been there long before she was born and she never thought to ask about it. It was kind of relic in front of which she passed every day without really paying attention.

"What's the painting about?" asked Eva

"It's The *Palais Sans-Souci* in all its glory!" said Caroline imitating the voice of her father.

The whole family burst laughing.

"My God! Blain was so passionate about the people and history of the North!" remembered M. Lebrun.

"Too bad we never had the chance to go there," said Dr. Lebrun. "He invited us many times."

Caroline's mind went in overdrive while her mother was speaking. The *Palais Sans-Souci* painting seemed to be as old as the one in her room. Could it be that in the back of the painting was hidden also a message or a clue of some kind?

"How would you feel if we change the frame of the painting?" Caroline asked abruptly. "I think the one that's in place now is not matching at all."

Her parents looked straight at her with puzzled faces. Even Eva looked at her wondering what was she thinking.

"Do you understand the value of the painting?" exclaimed her father. "It was painted in 1816! That's almost two centuries ago! You don't damage or change such masterwork in any way, young lady."

Eva who was drying her nail polish, stopped and came to Caroline's rescue.

"Uncle, I think Caroline just meant to say that maybe the painting is hiding something."

Caroline lifted her shoulders casually.

"Tonton Blain could well have forgotten to tell you something."

Mr. Lebrun looked at his daughter with astonished eyes. It was he who had been the right-hand of François Blain. He who had spent long afternoons talking with him about the files of the law firm, about his health problems, his fears and his frustrations. He was the one who has seen him grow old. It was in his arms that he took his last breath.

Caroline's father burst out laughing.

"Seriously... What exactly would the painting be hiding?" he asked.

"Is that why you broke the frame of the painting in your room?" pointed out his wife with a very calm voice.

"She did what?" cried out Caroline's father.

"We were just playing, dad, and the painting fell off the wall," replied Caroline with a trembling voice.

"That's no excuse. When are you going to show me that you're growing up? Well, go get the painting in your room. I'll keep it from now on with me so you girls can play as much as you want."

"*Timoun se moun fou* - Children are crazy people - really?" said Mrs. Lebrun while shaking her head.

Caroline was surprised but barely upset by her parent's reaction. On the contrary, she was now sure that there were things that they were unaware of themselves. For her, it was now impossible to ask them or even to let them know what she had in mind.

However, the clues were piling up and her cousin and her still could not put the puzzle together. First the painting in her room dated 1840 with a message in several copies telling her to continue looking for someone she did not know; then this novel which turned out to be the second step to take but of which she could not find the clue; and then this landscape painted in 1816.... What else was Tonton Blain hiding from them?

Chapter 6

hen Eva finally told her cousin that she had finished reading the remaining chapters of the novel and had not noticed anything, Caroline was both disappointed and intrigued. She could not understand why Tonton Blain had gone to so much trouble for nothing.

The second quarter exams were well underway. But more than the exams, a field trip was the main interest of the students. Eva was elected class president and was helping to prepare an outing to an old military fortress on the mountain called *Fort-Jacques*.

The last day of the exams, Caroline stayed out of it all because of a persistent migraine. She took refuge in the library on the first floor.

The library was practically empty except for three students who seemed captivated by a comic book and a lone boy in the very back of the room. The lone boy was Ludovic. He did not see her and she did not want any attention right then anyhow. This was not the first time she has seen him in front of that computer near the staff-only door. He was always locked in his thoughts and task. He seemed to be in a different world. Time to time, he would run his hands through his cinnamon-colored hair. The boyish charm and smile that made all the girls' hearts fluttered were changed to a stern look and determination. Caroline never thought of telling Natalie or Eva that she had often seen him in the library.

The bell rang. Caroline lifted her head painfully. She noticed Ludovic quickly shutting down the computer and separating a paper from a pile. He folded it and shoved it in his pocket. In his haste, the paper fell on the floor. Caroline pushed herself out of the chair, slowly walked until she got where her friend was standing. She picked up the papers and tried to catch Ludovic. But he was gone and they were not going to see each other the rest of the day. She decided to give him the paper later.

Caroline returned in class to take her last exam that she finished two hours later. The school yard was deserted. Several light winds kicked dirt and a sea of rolled-up paper in the school yard creating little twisters. As she walked through the front gate, Caroline saw Eva and Ludovic already there talking and sharing a bag of *papita* – a fried plantain snack. Natalie was not too far from them. She was eating her *fresko* with grenadine syrup.

"Next week, Caroline and I will come to your house so we can see some of those drawings," she was saying.

"Is she nuts?" thought Caroline while buying a *fresko* with coconut flavor. She knew that each year Natalie gets infatuated with some boy and usually it is to her detriment.

"Sorry, Nat," Caroline answered quickly. "We won't be home."

"Really? Where are you going?"

Caroline gave Ludovic a look suggesting her disapproval of any visit.

"Hey, Ludovic!" she said. "Why don't you bring some of your drawings to the field trip in *Fort-Jacques*?"

"I'll do one better. I'll bring my sketchbook and I'll draw your portrait, Natalie."

"You'll do my portrait?" asked Natalie.

"Of course... No worried. Ciao ladies! I have to be somewhere."

Caroline understood that her evening was not going to be a peaceful one. Natalie was going to call her every five minutes wanting to know if she noticed and interpreted every gesture, word, look that she believed suggested interest, and, of course, even love. She will proceed to discuss the ideal dresses and accessories for the portrait. Caroline already felt exhausted.

It was only when she got home later that day that Caroline noticed that she completely forgot to give Ludovic his note back.

The paper with a corner torn apart was a copy. With part of an image missing, a series of arrows were coming from it and pointing down to four names. Some dates were scribbled in red. Two names appeared clearly *Jacques-Victor Henry Espérance* and *Francès-Améthyste Espérance*. Caroline could barely read the last two names. She could only distinguish the words *Simon, An,* and *re.* And at the bottom of the note, she read the French sentence: *Dieu et ma cause* (God and my cause).

Caroline was completely shocked. She let the twirling paper fall on the marble tiles. She covered her mouth to muffle the sound of her surprise. Her migraine returned. She got up from her bed and called out loud her cousin who was downstairs.

"I'm on the phone!" cried out Eva.

"You must come NOW!"

Eva rushed upstairs expecting a catastrophic event. She found Caroline pacing around in the room frantically.

"What is it?"

"Sit down and read this."

Eva could not believe what Caroline was explaining to her. It has been a while since Ludovic and her were friends, but never she would have been able to imagine he was hiding such a secret. He has always been discreet with his family connections. What has been only known was that after the deaths of his father and grandfather, he has been living alone with his mother. He has never shown any distress, any melancholy, any sadness.

"How is Ludovic connected to all of this?" Eva asked.

"It's us who are meddling in all this."

"Yes. That's true... After all, Tonton Blain was just a friend to your grandfather and father while he was the brother of Ludovic's grandfather... He was his great uncle."

"Correct! I don't know any Francès-Améhyste but Jacques-Victor Henry are the complete name of my father. As for Tonton Blain his given names were François-Ferdinand."

"Francès-Améthyste...," asked Eva to herself. "I have a feeling I have seen this before."

Eva opened her school bag and took out her history book.

"Here it is: *Henry I, By the grace of God and the Constitution...*"

"Wait. Henry I? That's the name of King Henry Christophe."

"Yes. And Jacques-Victor Henry and Francès-Améthyste were his children."

"Did he have any other children?"

"Let me see…It says here François-Ferdinand and Anne-Athénaïre…"

Caroline took Ludovic's note. There were two other

names on the list. If the first name was completely erased, the other was starting with an A. Caroline looked again and again. Yes, it was evident:

"If Jacques-Victor and Francès-Améthyste Espérance are named after the children of Henry Christophe, why not her, Anne-Athénaïre…," she realized.

Caroline scratched her forehead. Something was missing. The novel Tonton Blain gave her should have contained a clue. The dedication did say that the novel was the second step.

Caroline looked straight at her cousin.

"Did you really read your part in the book?" she asked.

"Hmmm," Eva answered with a funny smile. "Not really…"

Caroline sighed. Now she understood why they could not find what they were searching for.

"Where did you stop?"

"In chapter 23 and I don't think that I finished reading it."

"Ok. Finish it and me, I will read chapter 24".

Determined to find the connection, Caroline left no time for her cousin to say anything back. She gave her the used copy and started to read the new one. Both girls were engrossed in their reading for a solid thirty minutes when Eva realized something new.

"Look at this! Here on page 350."

Caroline flipped the pages and did not notice anything.

"What is it? What did you find?" she asked anxiously while taking her cousin's copy from her.

Neatly tucked between the pages of the used book, there was a singular loose page with a message:

"Come my dear friend
One must not fear to say that
In circumstances like these, not even
Death will bury all these objects fashioned with such
Artful hands. They must find darkness and sleep in this world
Vivaciously. Strive to defend the cause of the widow
In pain in the foreign land. He has the list. You know the names. Go! I
Dare not leave my daughters in the cold and sadness…"

Eva looked at the new book. It did not have this page. Caroline surmised that Tonton Blain must have inserted it when he gave her the novel.

"*He has the list. You know the names...* Could this be Ludovic's list of names?" Caroline asked out loud to herself.

"Wait! Where's the note you found on the back of the painting?" Eva asked.

Caroline rushed to her treasure chest and gently unfolded the note. The girls spread it along with the loose paper, and the old book on Eva's bed.

"For sure, there is a link between these three things."

The girls reexamined each clue more closely and compared each word.

"Why is there a dash in the middle of the note from the painting?" asked Caroline abruptly.

"I don't think that has any meaning," answered Eva.

"I don't think so...," said Caroline. "In grammar, a dash between two words usually links them together."

Eva ripped a piece of paper from her chemistry notebook.

"I have an idea. Let's write down the word: *cause...lest...*"

"Uh?"

"Then, *Our Cause-lest*?"

"Really?" asked Caroline.

The two cousins burst out laughing. It was impossible to form a meaningful sentence with the words. However, the more Caroline looked, the more she wondered why the sentences of the message found behind her painting did not continue normally. The person who wrote them often went on the next line when it was least expected.

In turn, Caroline tore a sheet of paper from a notebook and write down the first word of each line.

"My; Arrived; Roaming; Imagine…"

Caroline stopped, shook her head:

"This makes no sense."

"Then, try each letter", suggested Eva.

Eva picked up the message and dictated the letters to her cousin:

"M… A… R… I… E… - L… O… U… I… S… E…"

"Woh! It's a poem in acrostic form," cried out Caroline.

MARIE-LOUISE… How had they not noticed it earlier? But who was she? Was she one of the women in the portrait? Caroline went to take her notebook with her family tree. She looked five generations back on both her father and her mother side. No woman had that first name

Caroline picked up the novel. Like the message, the words over the page inserted in it, should also mean something.

"Let's try again the same way."

"Ok. Go!" said her cousin

"C... O... I... D... A...V... I... D...."

"Oh my God!" screamed Eva. "Marie-Louise Coidavid Christophe! It's her!"

"Her who?" ask Caroline puzzled.

"The wife of Henry I!"

"So, the CC doesn't mean carbon copy...They are the Queen's initials!"

Caroline and Eva ran out of the room and down to the living room. They did not even notice Dr. Lebrun coming out of the TV room. They went straight to the wall where Mr. Lebrun hanged both the *Palais Sans-Souci* painting and the portraiture of the three women.

Caroline and Eva slowly walked toward the artistic pieces, fascinated by the look in the eyes of the three women. Royal in their silky garbs, the dignified smile of the figure in the middle pointed to a queenly distinction.

"She must be the queen Marie-Louise and the two others Francès-Améthyste and Anne-Athénaïre."

"The *Palais Sans-Souci* was their home…"

Chapter 7

he day for the field trip arrived. The students were waiting eagerly in the school's yard. Teachers, students, and staff were dressed leisurely.

"Well," Eva said, "he won all the Oscars!"

The colors that Mr. Alexandre was wearing attracted all attentions. With a washed blue jean, the teachers had a fluorescent green t-shirt, a brown pull-over around the waste, and a white cap. The girls could not help but laughing at the sight. It was almost like watching a peacock in its natural habitat. Mr. Alexandre for good measure was also carrying a backpack and had a camera around his neck.

It was soon time to go. Students, teachers, and staff boarded the two buses that would bring them to Kenscoff. Caroline and Eva were in Mr. Alexandre's bus and Natalie went to the other vehicle. All were seated, but the driver could not depart. Some students were running late.

"We're going to wait fifteen more minutes," said the teacher standing next to the bus driver.

It so happens that one of the expected students was Ludovic.

"Where is he?" asked Caroline.

"He did say he would come," answered Eva.

Caroline had so much to share, compare, and ask Ludovic. She was eager to hear what stories his grandfather and great-uncle told him. She was eager to see what artifacts they may have given him.

The buses finally left without Ludovic. The students were relieved. The heat inside the vehicle was starting to rise. Sitting at the window, Caroline opened her backpack and pulled out tissue to wipe her forehead. She was happy to have done her usual bun. Eva who had her hair down, was now fixing it up. Caroline took a pin out of her hair and passed it on to her.

The bus seats were uncomfortable, but the excitement of the students was translated into songs, laughter, and jokes. Time to time, an over enthusiastic student was reminded to sit and buckle up.

Whitin a half-hour, the buses were leaving Port-au-Prince behind and were climbing toward Pétion-Ville. The road became smaller and was zigzagging in the mountain.

The ride that will bring them to Kenscoff took over a couple of hours. Gradually the hubbub of the city gave way to the peaceful view of the surrounding mountains. The air was getting cooler. Caroline who was singing with other students could feel now the pressure in her ears.

They were getting closer to Kenscoff.

The dean of students thought it was the right time to remind the students of a few rules.

"Your attention, please. We are group 1 and the other bus is group 2. Mr. Alexandre will be your tour guide. The person near you is your companion for the day. Stay together and do not leave your group. I hope everyone has brought their lunch because no one will be allowed to leave and go buy anything. And please, pick up after yourselves."

"Sir! At Kenscoff there are some good *fritay* (fried food) merchants. Would it be possible to stop to buy something?" asked a student from the back of the bus.

"No," said the dean with a very serious face. "We will not stop for any reason. You were all told to bring your lunches with you. If and I say if there are at the locations some small merchants, you will be able to buy what they sell only. The rules will be strictly enforced. We want you to have a safe and satisfactory outing. So, please follow the rules and enjoy yourselves!"

The momentarily interruption caused by the dean's remarks quickly faded. The students exploded in shouts and laughter. The busses left the paved road and took a dirt road that brought them to a parking space. Once they stopped, the students quickly exited the buses. Caroline and Eva stretched their legs.

From afar, they could see Natalie making her way to them. She wasn't wearing the clothes that Caroline and her agreed on after hours spent over the phone discussing about the right outfit.

"Ludovic is not here?" she asked.

"Well, no," answered Eva.

"How come?"

"How would we know, Nat?" said Caroline.

Just like her cousin, Caroline too was starting to get annoyed by her friend's obsession for Ludovic. It was Mr. Alexandre who came to remind Natalie that she should stay with her group who finally put an end to the conversation.

"Listen kids", said the teacher. "There are two sites we're going to visit: *Fort-Alexandre* and *Fort-Jacques*. Our group will visit first Fort Jacques and the other Fort Alexandre further down. Later we'll make the switch."

Mr. Alexandre's voice echoed in the surrounding pine forest. Accompanying the human voices, the birds occasionally would be heard. Caroline closed her eyes for a moment and took in the crisp and clean fresh air of the mountains. An accentuated odor of pine cones permeated the cool air. The rays of a soft sun darted though the branches of the pines. A feeling of calm and well-being invaded her body.

"As you know," continued the teacher, "the day that followed the declaration of independence in 1804, Dessalines felt the need to protect the country from a possible comeback of the French army. This is why, in March of the same year, he passed an order to the commanders of the three *departments* (provincial regions) to raise fortifications at the top of the highest mountains."

As the students were following him, the teacher entered the fort through a rotting wooden door. The group then climbed a small stone staircase that led them to the roof. Mr. Alexandre headed straight for the cannon facing the sky. After a few steps, the group stopped. A stunning sight unfolded in front of Caroline and the others. From the fort she had a panoramic view from east to west stretching from the plains of Cul-de-Sac near the border with the Dominican Republic to the bay of Port-au-Prince that was sparkling under the clear blue sky.

"Here," indicated Mr. Alexandre "we are standing above three thousand feet high on the mountain *Montagne de la Selle.* As you can see, from where Fort Jacques is situated, it was easy to see the enemy coming from many directions."

"Sir, how many forts like these are there in the country?" asked Caroline.

"Well, about thirty in different sizes. And not just any kind. In fact, in a very short time, the Haitians would erect the most extraordinary fortification system that the American continent had known at the time."

Caroline looked around her. She could not believe that a building built nearly two centuries ago weathered the times so well. The stone walls, the doors, the cannons, everything exuded the human genius of a time when construction machinery was still at its infancy.

"Obviously," continued Mr. Alexandre, "none of these forts are comparable to the *Citadelle Laferrière.*"

"Yes, *pitit tan m* (my dear child)!" said a student in the typical Creole spoken in the northern part of the country.

The staff searched for the taunting student. But it was a waste of time. All the children were laughing. Eva suddenly pulled Caroline closer and whispered in her ear:

"I completely forgot: Redingote is originally from Cap-Haitian."

"No joke!" said Caroline.

Now Caroline understood why Mr. Alexandre sounded so passionate every time he referenced Cap-Haitian.

Mr. Alexandre downplayed the reaction of the students and continued leading lively the trip.

"Now we will enter the fort. And please, pay attention. A surprise awaits you."

The laughter stopped and the students followed the teacher down a rock-paved path. Soon they found themselves in the enclosure around a pool facing an entrance in the stone wall.

"Get a little closer, children. Do you see this opening? It's a secret passage that allowed soldiers to escape to Fort Alexandre below. Thus, they could escape without being seen from the outside."

Mr. Alexandre took the lead of the group and the amazed students followed him. They ducked and entered one after the other in an arch-shaped stone tunnel that would lead them to Fort Alexandre.

Natalie's group had already finished their visit when Caroline and Eva joined her. There were a few picnic tables and they were already taken. Natalie took a sheet from her bag and spread it on the grass between the trees. She barely finished setting up that Caroline threw herself on it.

"Man! That was a long walk!" she said.

"At least," replied Natalie, "it wasn't in the heat."

Not far from Caroline, Eva joined also some of her classmates who were stretching out on the grass. A battery-powered radio was playing the latest hits. Their lunch was a few bottles of juice and enough sandwiches to feed a regiment.

Suddenly, Caroline bursts out laughing.

"What's wrong?" ask Natalie who was eating some cookies.

Not too far from them, a few girls were playing a strange ball game. Divided into two, each group tried to catch the ball without touching the trees around them. Caroline found the idea amusing. She hurried to finish her lunch to support the team of her choice. A few minutes later, more students joined in.

The air was filled with screams and laughter. Mr. Alexandre got closer and took some pictures of the game. Then a few native birds attracted his attention and drew him away. Caroline could not stop watching him. Since her cousin told her that the teacher was from the Cap, an avalanche of questions was rushing to her mind.

Mr. Alexandre was now alone and Caroline felt it the right time for her to talk to him. After wildly gesturing to attract Eva's attention, Caroline finally was able to make her leave the game.

"We have to talk to Redingote now," she said to her while walking towards the teacher. "Maybe there are things he can tell us."

"Do you know what you're going to ask him?" said Eva in a low tone of voice.

Caroline shrugged. She was not too sure.

"Excuse us, Mr. Alexandre," said Caroline. "We wanted to say thank you for your guided tour."

Mr. Alexandre stopped for a moment to take pictures.

"You're welcome," he replied.

"My cousin and I would like to visit the *Citadelle Laferrière* one day."

"Oh, you will like it! Do you have family there?

"Uh…no."

"Then you will absolutely have to stay at *L'Hotel de la Couronne*."

"Why?" asked Eva puzzled.

"This hotel was built at the beginning of the 20th century. It was inspired by the original Coidavid's hotel."

Caroline gulped and exchanged a surprised look with her cousin.

"In the past, the *Hotel de la Couronne* was an inn that belonged to the parents of Marie-Louise Coidavid."

"You mean, Henry Christophe's wife?" asked Caroline.

"Yes. The inn was well known in Cap-François as it was named before the reign of Henry Christophe. The king later called the city Cap-Henry. Obviously, the Hotel de la Couronne is not the same as the one we have now."

While speaking, the teacher pointed to a stone wall where he wanted to sit.

"As it was in the past, this inn extends over a vast domain with a magnificent garden and fruit trees. There is a small art gallery at the end of the garden where artisans from the nearby area exhibit their work of art. There are folk dance shows and trips to historic sites. It is a popular tourist destination renown all around the world."

As the teacher described the ambiance in the Hotel de la Couronne of the Coidavids, Caroline's imagination went into overdrive. She saw herself in the skin of young Marie-Louise walking through the corridors and gardens of the inn, conversing with customers, and having fun with other young people of her age. While she was living that alternate reality, she heard Eva's voice asking a question:

"Marie-Louise was an emancipated slave?"

"Not at all. Marie-Louise was born free. Her parents were born as slaves and were freed before she was born. Her father wanted the finest of educations for her. He sent her to school and encouraged her to take music and art lessons."

"At that time," said Caroline, "a young freed woman could have been like us."

"Not exactly. An over educated black woman could have trouble finding a husband. Remember we are talking about colonial times. For that reason, Marie-Louise's mother did not really like her husband pushing their daughter in this direction. She managed to keep her grounded. She related to her all the sufferings they experienced as a slave and forced her to show respect and consideration for those who worked for them on their estate."

A sound from whistle caught the attention of Caroline and her cousin.

"Gather your things!" announced the dean in the distance.

"Comme on girls!" said Mr. Alexandre. "It's time to leave."

Chapter 8

The return to Port-au-Prince was less lively. Eva and many other students were dozing off. Caroline watched the landscape pass by. Exerts of the message was coming to her mind. She remembered clearly this one: *Strive to defend the cause of the widow in pain in the foreign land.*

What could this sentence mean? Caroline sighed a little and looked at the history teacher. Although seated in the same row as she, he was busy joking with the driver and another teacher.

When Mr. Alexandre finally leaned back in his seat, Caroline looked at him straight in the eye and smiled.

"Sir, it's very nice what you told us about the Hotel de la Couronne. But I would like to ask something else."

"Go ahead," encouraged the teacher.

"Did Queen Marie-Louise lived and suffered in a foreign country?"

Caroline's question puzzled Mr. Alexandre. It was very rare that people were so interested in this queen. Since the death of the king, she was hardly the subject of any conversation. She did not figure very much in history books. The teacher stared at the young girl for a moment as if he did not know where to start.

"Yes. Very much so," he finally answered with a deep voice.

"What happened?"

"Well, after the death of King Henry Christophe and his son, the crowned prince, the lives of both the Queen and her daughters were in danger. President Boyer first offered them his protection in Port-au-Prince before they decided to go into exile in England."

England? Was this the country the note was talking about? Was it where she *landed so many years* later? Was that why the message said *nothing looks like ours*?

"But it's a cold place," said Caroline.

"Cold and damp. The queen and her daughters arrived there at the beginning of autumn and very quickly winter followed. Instead of the inviting warmth of tropical nature of Cap-Haitian, they saw the leaves of trees turning yellow and red, the weather turning rainy and cold. The food they were accustomed to became exotic and hard to find. Still in mourning, they were experiencing both a culture shock and climate shock. Adding to these helpless circumstances, one of her daughters suffered from asthma and her condition quickly deteriorated. The queen herself suffered from rheumatism and with the winter it got worse. And, don't forget, she was queen in her country with all the privileges that her status brought. But there, she and her daughters became simply foreigners who had to survive in a place, in a world they did not know or were accustomed to."

Caroline never visited a country where it was so cold. But Eva's parents who often called told them how in Canada in autumn and winter the temperature could drop sharply. Caroline shook her head. She did not understand the queen's choice.

"Why did they choose Europe and not a Caribbean or Latin American country? The climate is the same as ours over there and we eat almost the same food."

"Well… Don't forget that we're talking about 1821. Beside Haiti, no other country in the area had yet abolished slavery. No country had yet declared their independence. But in Europe, despite racism, it was amid the Industrial Revolution. The Royal family had savings there and friends they could count on."

Caroline remembered studying the Industrial Revolution when she was in 9th grade. It was a time where a series of inventions were happening in Europe and setting new milestone in the world.

"Fortunately, the queen had her daughters," said Caroline.

"You would think," replied the teacher.

"Why do you say that, sir?"

"Because only a few years after their departure from Haiti, both of her two daughters died. She was left alone for a long time before she too died."

Suddenly, Caroline felt the deep sorrow of this queen - mourning, cold, exile, loneliness. What misfortunes! Yes, as the message said, she had indeed been *the widow in pain in the foreign land…*

The buses were arriving at the school. Mr. Alexandre passed his camera around his neck, ready to get out. Caroline woke up Eva. Briefly she told her what the teacher revealed to her.

Once home, both girls run to the phone and called Ludovic. The phone rang and rang without anyone answering. They kept redialing until finally, Ludovic picked up.

"Are you ok?" Eva asked. "We haven't seen you today."

"I woke up too late this morning. But I'm okay. I had things to do anyway. How was the trip?"

"Super great. You were the only one missing. We have a few things to tell you. Could you meet us at home?"

"Why?"

"We can't tell you over the phone. When you get here, we will explain to you."

"I can't now. Maybe tomorrow."

Caroline smiled. If only Ludovic knew what she had to tell him, he would have rushed to her house. She had information that he would want to know. She knew the answers to many questions he has probably been asking. Luckily, she was there in the library the day he lost the paper! Otherwise, someone else would have picked it up and all that information would be lost forever.

It was almost eleven o'clock when the two cousins woke up the next day. Caroline was eager to meet Ludovic because she wanted to find out his understanding of the whole story.

"Do you think," asked Eva, "that the queen wrote the message?"

"Sure. Except that I don't know what we should continue to look for."

Caroline got up and tiptoed to her desk. From a pile of drawings and watercolors, she retrieved a notebook and a pen. She went back to her bed and then got in her warm sheets. Both girls began to write down all the clues they had found.

A knock on their bedroom door stopped them in their quest. Mrs. Lebrun stuck her head through the door.

"Still having your beauty sleep? I'm leaving for the supermarket in thirty minutes. I would like you two to come with me. Caroline I'm going to meet someone you have not seen you in a long time. Hurry up girls!"

Caroline pouted. This was not how she had imagined her Sunday morning. They already plotted how they were going to approach Ludovic about the discovery of his paper at the library and so forth. Now, they would have to wait longer to speak to him.

Caroline pulled her sheets up to her face and covered her head. Eva snatched them from her and pulled her out of the bed. Caroline almost twisted her ankle while putting her feet on the floor without paying attention to all the school books laying around. They were searching for a drawing like the one that was on Ludovic's paper.

Both parents were already waiting in the car for the girls. Mr. Lebrun blew the horn. Caroline and her cousin ran down the stairs straight to the driveway.

"We haven't had breakfast yet!" complained Eva.

"Get in, girls," Caroline's father replied. "We'll buy something at the bakery. "

Caroline and Eva did not have to wait long. The bakery was fifteen minutes away. Like every Sunday the tiny shop was packed. The line of customers almost reached the street. It was renowned for its *mille-feuilles* (napoleon) topped with cream, its crusty baguettes and its *pâtés* that melted in the mouth. Caroline's father took a few pâtés filled with cod fish and some other ones filled with ground beef. Her mother and Eva added some small fruit pies and onion pies. Caroline could not decide. Her nose up against the glass-panels, she breathed in the smells of the pastries. Her eyes widened at the specials of the day. She wanted to take a bit of everything, but she ended up ordering chocolate croissants, a vanilla *éclair* and two *mille-feuilles*.

Once in the car, Caroline opened her box and smelled the pastries' delicious perfume. Then, she grabbed a croissant. With a reflecting gaze brought on by the deliciousness of the croissant, she looked at the bustling humanity on the streets. All these people, inside all these houses, there are stories, there are secrets to discover, to be revealed. Now, one such story touched her and family at a personal level and she was fortunate to have discovered it, to have somewhat lived it in all its sadness and beauty.

The sound of her mother's pager pulled her out of her day dream.

"Oh dear," she said in an annoyed tone. "I have to get to a phone. It's important."

Mr. Lebrun without saying a word made a U-turn and returned to the bakery to allow his wife to find a phone. As they waited in the car, a street vendor who sold flashlights approached them. Caroline's father opened the glove box and checked if he had already replaced the broken one. The glove box was empty.

While her father was haggling with the merchant on various items, the girls, seated in the back, were sharing their pastries. Normally Eva did not like *éclairs*; but, after tasting one of Carolina's, she found it very delicious. The cousins then bartered an *éclair* for a fruit pie. Mrs. Lebrun came back in the car with an annoyed face.

"I can't wait when we finally have a cell phone," she said. "I could have just called that patient without having to come back here."

"Soon, honey!" said her husband tenderly.

Caroline made a victory gesture. Finally, her parents were going to catch up with the rest of the world. That box her dad was carrying on his belt will be gone. No more seeing her mother digging like crazy in her big purse to find hers. And then, she too, would finally be able to talk to whoever she wanted, wherever she wanted.

"What are you going to do with your beepers?" Eva asked.

"Well," replied Mr. Lebrun, "it seems that soon beepers will be something of the past."

"Oh yes!" agreed Caroline. "You can do anything with cell phones. Natalie's parents already have one. She and Ti Boul will have theirs by the summer."

"Ti Boul… Redingote… What are those names?" her mother asked with a smile.

"Ah…," said Caroline. "Now you see why I don't like it when you call me Linou in public."

"So, you're complaining about Linou, when we almost named you Anne Francès-Améthyste Athénaïre!" Caroline's mother retorted amusingly.

Caroline nearly chocked on a croissant when she heard her mother uttering that name. And Eva was frozen with surprised. It was as if suddenly time stopped.

"Careful," said Caroline's mother as she handed her a bottle of water.

"Who wanted to call me by that name?"

"The same one who named your father Jacques-Victor Henry…"

"Tonton Blain?" cried out Caroline in astonishment.

"But why?" Eva asked.

"Because" Caroline's father replied, "for him it was an illustrious name. "

Caroline's mind was spinning like crazy. She took a sip of water to moisten her throat dried up by emotion.

Yes, all the names on Ludovic's list now had a face. And she, Caroline, knew them all.

Chapter 9

t was in the afternoon that Ludovic finally came to Caroline's house. He arrived almost at the time when the family was returning home. He greeted the girl's parents before letting himself be guided under the pergola. Ludovic's shorts and t-shirt were streaked with various colors. Caroline stared at him. Splashes of paint were on his face, on his hair, and on his muscular arms.

"What took you so long?" reproached Eva.

"I'm doing a fresco in my room," explained Ludovic.

"A fresco in your room?" wondered Caroline. "And your mom is ok with that?"

"Yeah," answered Ludovic who did not understand Caroline's astonishment.

"Cool," Eva said.

Caroline met Ludovic's mother just once, when they dropped him off at his house after school. Almost as tall as her son, she looked so proud of him.

"Lucky you," added Caroline. "My mother would never allow such a thing. But what are you painting exactly?"

"A faux stone wall."

"Interesting," said Eva. "You'll have to show it to us when you're done."

"For sure…"

The trio walked toward the pergola.

"So, what do you girls have to talk to me about?"

Caroline took a deep breath and hesitated, not knowing where to start. Then, finally she began to tell the entire story – from finding the note behind her painting to the name she should have had.

Caroline saw in Ludovic's face a strange mix of frustration and astonishment. He just spent two whole days moving heaven and earth to find his paper. He knew he tuck it in his pocket when he left the library. He did not understand how and when he lost it. He looked through his schoolbag several times. He ran through and turned inside out his shirt and pants. He even thought he had left it in the taxi that took him home that day. He finally accepted the idea he lost it forever.

"Sorry, Ludo," said Caroline. "I wanted to tell you but you weren't answering my calls."

"It's ok... Could I have it back?" he said with a serious tone.

Caroline went to her room and then returned almost immediately. Ludovic looked at the paper.

"Hmmm...," he let out before bursting into laughter.

Both Caroline and her cousin looked at him, not knowing how to interpret this sudden reaction.

"What's the matter?" Eva asked.

"My father had the same first names as your uncle."

"Really?" wondered Caroline. "And who gave him those names?"

"My grand-father."

So, thought Caroline, the two brothers spent their life making sure that everyone had the same first names. Apparently, a competition each side was determined to win. What were they trying to do?

"And who else in your family has the names of the king's children?"

"Nobody. Anyway, not to my knowledge."

Ludovic leaned against the railing of the pergola and took a deep breath as he folded his paper.

"Listen, I know that François Blain was my uncle. Maybe he had a funny sense of humor. And I think he played a trick on you Caro."

"Nope. I don't think so," said Caroline with conviction. "Otherwise, he wouldn't have told my father as well to defend the cause or to keep what he gave him tirelessly."

"Then he played a trick on your father too."

Caroline frowned. She knew Tonton Blain was not the type to play such tricks. She did not understand why Ludovic was trying to downplay her discoveries.

"Impossible," she said." My painting and my father's painting are both originals from the 19th century. These are authenticated pieces."

"And what about yours?" asked Eva to Ludovic. "When were they painted?"

"Which paintings?"

"You don't have any paintings at home?" asked Eva.

"Uh… Nothing interesting like the ones you guys have."

Caroline and Eva looked at each other feeling a little bit lost. Then, what cause Ludovic's paper was telling him to defend?

"Where did you find your paper?" Caroline asked in disbelief.

Ludovic paused. He never shared his secret with anyone, not even his mother. But now, with everything that has been discovered, he had no choice.

"I found it behind a mirror."

"A mirror?" Eva asked.

"My grandfather had a large mirror framed in carved wood and decorated with golden leaf. He always told us that it was a family heirloom. Since my mom was his only daughter-in-law, she thought he would eventually give it to her. But before dying, he decided to put it in my bedroom and he made me swear never to give it to anyone, no matter what. So, I kept it until last year."

"What happened?"

"I was rearranging my room and I wanted to move the mirror. As I lifted it, a small screw in the back hurt my finger. I was about to remove it and that's when a yellow paper fell out. It had the drawing and all the names you saw on it."

"So, your grandfather knew it was there," said Caroline.

"Yes. And that's when I understood why he made me swear not ever give it away."

So, thought Caroline, Mr. Paul and his bother knew something. They were trying to find a way to hide it

"On your paper, there are several surnames. And next to them, there are some dates. What does that mean?" asked Caroline.

"It seems that they are the names of important Cap-Haitian families. And the dates are their birth year. Simon was born in 1826, Jacques-Victor Espérance in 1849 and so on."

"Do you know who these people are?" Eva asked.

"Probably members of my family, although my mother does not know them."

"What about the picture?"

"I don't know yet."

Ludovic crossed his arms over his chest. He has been trying to understand his paper for more than three years. Three years since his grandfather died. Three long years where he had been going from internet café to internet café to find an explanation. After such a lengthy search Ludovic was convinced, he exhausted all paths to the mystery. But he went ahead and asked Caroline:

"I would like to see your paper."

"Oh, okay," said Caroline. "Let me go get it."

"Would you like something to drink?" asked Eva.

"Just a glass of water. Thanks"

While waiting for the water, Ludovic lifted his head and looked at the sky. The typical drought of this time of the year was coming to an end. Gray clouds were gathering in the sky. A flock of *Boustabak* bird was flying over his head and made themselves known with their shrill cries. From the back porch, Eva called Ludovic to join her.

"It's going to rain soon," she told him while handing him the glass of water. "I don't want to get my hair wet."

Caroline was back. She passed the novel to Eva as she carefully opened her note. Ludovic came close to the two girls. They all sat by a table and examined Caroline's message in his hands.

But suddenly, Ludovic's face turned pale. Stunned, unable to utter a word, his mouth stayed wide opened. This cursive, thin, slender, delicate, and nervous handwriting was the same in his own original document.

Chapter 10

aroline was so certain that Ludovic's paper had revealed everything. But the young man just told them that the top part of his paper did not show on the photocopy because of the irregular format of the original.

The girls were completely shocked. They did not dare to place a word, even move.

"And what does it say?" Eva finally asked Ludovic.

"*Thus begins our Family Tree...*"

Caroline was puzzled by the sentence. No one in the Lebrun's family tree was named Simon or Espérance. She also did not remember Tonton Blain ever mentioning these names in his family.

"Not long ago, my mother wanted to get rid of a few books. They were some of my grandfather's books. One particularly described a few important families calling Cap-Haitian home. And these family names were among them but the book did not give any details. It seems that they were very well-known clans. I tried to ask my mother, but she didn't know much."

"Man!" said Caroline.

"Were you able to find what the drawing represents?" Eva asked.

"No."

"Maybe we can find something on the internet," suggested Caroline.

"I've tried," said Ludovic. "I've spent hours looking and there's nothing."

"Where do you think we could go?" asked Caroline.

"At the *Bibliothèque Nationale* (National Public Library)" suggested Ludovic. "This is my last chance. I have a membership. "

Caroline's mother came out of the house and looked at the sky. A few droplets of rain were now falling on the dirt ground.

"It's time to get inside."

The children followed her into the kitchen. The cook was frying *marinad* (a flavorful batter), plantains, *akra* (a taro batter) and some sausage.

"Tonight, it's *fritay* (fried food) night!" said Caroline's mother. "Do you like that, Ludovic?"

"Yes, I love that. Thank you, Dr. Lebrun," said the young man.

"Then indulge!"

Caroline's father put a few paper plates and some bottles of soda on the table. Caroline rushed first toward the *akra* which she quickly devours with appetite. They were made to perfection: spicy and soft on the inside and crispy on the outside. Caroline hugged the cook who smiled widely, happy that her cooking was appreciated. Between the *akra* bites, Caroline informed her parents:

"We need to do research for our history class; so, we have to go to the *Bibliothèque Nationale.*"

"What?" cried out her mother. "You want to go downtown alone? You want to get mugged?!"

"Mom, our school *is* located downtown."

Mr. Lebrun pouted as he put a little *pikliz* (spicy coleslaw) on his plate.

"The girls are only going to the library, Micheline." he said.

Caroline's mother took one of the *marinad* the cook had just taken out of the frying pan, blew on it several times before putting a small piece in her mouth.

"You can't do your research at school?" she asked without paying attention to her husband sentence.

"Mom, what we need is neither at school nor on the Internet. And, we won't be alone, Ludovic will come with us."

As she spoke, Caroline gave a distressed look to her father. Mr. Lebrun touched her shoulder to calm her down.

"Honey", her father said to her mother, "the solution is simple: I have an appointment downtown this Tuesday, I'll take them."

It was the first time that Caroline and her cousin were going to the public library. And so, the trio was dropped off in front of the building. Mr. Lebrun informed them that they will be picked up in two hours. Caroline got out of the car first. She stood in front of the glass building highlighted in white paint. Between the palm trees which adorned the entrance, Caroline saw a plaque at the bottom of the wall. It mentioned 1940 as the construction date of the library. This date alone made her heart beat faster. She knew that by opening the glass door, she would immediately step into the past. Ludovic hastened to open the front door for the two cousins.

The library opened to a massive building from the inside. The lady at a counter made sure they understood that they needed to leave their bags behind before going any further. Eva took out a notebook and a pencil box out of her bag. The lady exchanged the bags for a reference number.

A large chandelier majestically dangled in the middle of the high ceiling. Dozens of tables were arranged in rows side by side in the middle of the large room. People of all ages were researching or confirming a story or simply reading a book. Only the noise of fans or a few footsteps broke the stillness of the room from time to time.

"Where do you think we should start?" Caroline asked in a low voice.

"With the newspapers," said Ludovic. "There is always a lot of information there."

That was true. The oldest running daily newspaper in the country started back in the 19th century.

"No. The volumes by Thomas Madiou would be better. They are the definitive reference for Haitian history. We should start with them," suggested Eva.

"Let's go for Thomas Madiou !" said Ludovic.

The party walked up to the librarian. A thin, gray-haired, tall man silently greeted them.

"We would like to see some books by Thomas Madiou, please." said Ludovic.

"Which one?" asked the man sternly in a low tone.

"Uh… those that talk about Henry Christophe."

"These books should only be in the rare books section."

The friends followed the man into a space reserved for rare copies.

"Wait here," the man told them nonchalantly before disappearing into a prohibited room.

Compared to the main hall, the rare books section was in a tiny space. A handful of people were consulting old newspapers under the supervision of a young woman. A particular smell of old papers filled the room. Caroline could not help but stare, fascinated by the way the researchers were giving the old publications all their attention.

"We only have Volume VI for the moment," said the returning man. "As soon as you're done, give it back to the lady sitting over there."

The book was big. Ludovic placed it on the table. Caroline and Eva moved their chairs closer to him. All three felt like they were looking into a slice of history and their lives depended on it. One page after another, they began to analyze the content.

"We not going to read all 500 pages, right?" interposed Eva. "The period covered begins just before the year of the king's death."

"You're right," Caroline told her. "The portrait of the queen dates from 1840. What we need must be after 1820."

Ludovic barely paid attention to Caroline's arguments and continued his search through the pages.

"It seems that at the beginning of each section, there is a summary of what the author is going to talk about," he noticed. "Maybe we should try looking there…"

Yet, every page was a disappointment. The author was only referring, so far, to the inner workings of the kingdom.

"Let's see," said Caroline "if there are any images that could match your drawing."

Caroline did not yet finish her sentence when she came across an image representing two coins. One of the two minted effigies featured a crown and the image of a crowned bird while the other displayed the face of a man.

"My coins!" said Caroline and Ludovic at the same time.

Over her glasses, the lady at the back of the room looked up at the overexcited teenagers. She frowned and cleared her throat signaling to them to keep quiet. Caroline gave her a silly smile.

"Wow!" whispered Ludovic. "Do you have the same ones?"

"Yes, and others like them," said Caroline while pointing at a picture.

The images were exactly like some of Caroline's coins. *Henrycus Dei Gratia Haiti Rex. 1811* said the face while the back read: *Deus. Causa. Atque Gladius Meus L'An 8.*

"Let me see," said Eva pulling the book towards her.

"*Deus... Causa,*" repeated Caroline.

"God and my Cause," Ludovic told her with a happy smile.

Beside his drawing, it was the first time that Ludovic was seeing this inscription. Caroline held on to one of his muscular arms, while Eva was gripping the other.

"You see, Caro. I told you to make a bracelet out of them."

"And I told you that I don't want to have my arm cut off."

"Hey, listen to this!" said Ludovic with his eyes on the book. *The Palais Sans-Souci was plundered. The pictures, the furniture, the mirrors, everything was smashed; the wardrobe of the King, that of the Queen, those of the Princesses and Princes were taken and carried away... Richard and the other officers seized from La Ferrière lots of money...*"

"Do you think that our paintings and the mirror come from the loot?" asked Caroline.

"What do you mean? My grandfather wasn't a thief," retorted Ludovic angrily.

Caroline and Eva were silent at first, both surprises by his reaction.

"That's not what I meant Ludo. But just think about this: we have the coins, I have two paintings from 1800, you have a mirror from the same period, a message from the queen, two brothers telling us to defend a cause, AND what we just read... Don't you think that's a lot of coincidences?"

Caroline was right. All their research were bringing them closer to the king. All roads were leading to the cause that had to be defended. That cause was now expanding in every direction.

Ludovic ran his hand through his hair.

"My grandfather's family must have known something about all of this. But the last time I saw them, I was just a baby."

"What about your mom?" ask Eva. "Does she know where they live in Cap-Haitian?

"No. It's been a long time since she spoke with them. She lost contact with them."

"Hm... So, your grandfather never talked about this list or anything like that?" asked Caroline.

"If I remember well, he did mention the coins that were part of his collection of old money; but he never told me anything else."

"You know what?" Eva said. "If Redingote knows so much about the life of Marie-Louise Christophe, I am sure he will be able to tell us who are these officers who looted the *Citadelle*."

Chapter 11

The following Monday, like every Monday, the two hours of history class was ended by recess. Mr. Alexandre was gathering his books when Caroline and Ludovic came up to him.

"I understand that a large group of students are planning to go with you to Cap-Haitian."

"I really don't know, Mr. Alexandre. It might just be Ludovic and my family. But I still have a few questions…"

The teacher stared at them in puzzlement. Marie-Louise Coidavid was not the only queen of Haiti. Anacaona was also been a queen and the history books always highlighted her as a worthy personage. However, Marie-Louise was rarely the subject of conversations. Additionally, his students are hardly interested in studying the past. But this year, there were not only one, but three who wanted to know everything about events that were over a century old.

"You all have such a fascination for this period... What exactly are you looking for?"

The direct question was unexpected.

"Well sir, we want to visit the *Citadelle* during the summer. We want to have the full experience of history," answered Caroline.

"Okay. That's nice to hear," said the teacher mechanically. "Right now, I don't have time. But at 1pm, we can meet in front of the teacher's lounge."

Caroline and Ludovic went to the cafeteria and quickly ordered two sandwiches and two bottles of soda. Then they went outside and sat under an almond tree facing the cafeteria. They needed to discuss what they were going to ask the teacher.

While they were talking and eating lunch, Caroline's eyes met Natalie's. She was looking through the cafeteria's windows with an inquisitive gaze on her face. Caroline waved at her, but she looked away visibly upset.

When they returned from recess, Caroline felt something has changed in Natalie. Her gestures were abrupt. She was grumpy. She could barely talk to her. She was mumbling incomprehensibly. Caroline did not put too much weight to that. Her friend was known for her mood swings; and surely, she was in one of those moods right now. Caroline knew it was best to leave her alone.

Caroline sat down and opened her science notebook. On a page, in the middle of the dizzying formulas, she began to finish a drawing she started earlier. She knew that the science teacher was going to be late as always. Caroline jumped a little when Natalie suddenly spoke to her from behind.

"You guys are great friends lately."

Caroline did not know what her friend was hinting at. Natalie grabbed her backpack angrily and moved to another seat on the other side of the room.

"Traitor!" she threw at Caroline.

Throughout the rest of the day, Caroline struggled to find an explanation for Natalie's words. But finally, she understood that her friend was mad at her, but the reason for that still eluded her.

When the final bell rung, Ludovic went to get Eva in order to meet Mr. Alexandre. Meanwhile, Caroline went to see Natalie. A few students, who noticed the exchange earlier, hanged around the room. They didn't want to miss what was going to happen next.

"What's wrong?" Caroline asked quietly.

"So, you like him!" Natalie burst out. "You think you could fool me by pretending that you don't care about him?"

For a few seconds, Caroline tried to identify who that "him" was. To her knowledge, she was not playing any kind of game regarding anyone. She paused a moment, and, suddenly, burst out laughing. She realizing who her friend was referring to. Natalie's anger exploded.

"Yeah… Play innocent! You think I didn't see your little game!"

"Natalie, I swear it's not what you think!"

"What is it then?"

"I don't have the time to tell you right now. But…"

"I don't need your gibberish! You can keep him to yourself!"

Ludovic was a handsome boy with a great personality, but he was just a friend - almost a brother with whom Caroline shared a secret. Caroline tried to find out what could have made Natalie have such a thought. She was saddened by this misunderstanding. But she was running out of time. She had to meet with Mr. Alexandre. She threw her bookbag on her shoulder and without adding anything more, walked away crestfallen.

Eva, Ludovic, and Caroline arrived at the teacher's lounge at the same time. Upon seeing them, Mr. Alexandre was surprised they remembered the appointment and kept their word.

"Well, well, well. This trip is a serious business…"

The teacher pointed to a few empty chairs to them.

"So, what would you like to know today?"

"Are you aware of a treasure that Henry Christophe hid at *Laferrière*?" Caroline asked straight away.

"So, it's this myth that interests you! Well, you are not alone. Many people after the king's death searched for this treasure."

"But, it's not a myth, sir," said Eva. "The other day, I read in Thomas Madiou's book that this treasure was taken away by some officers."

Mr. Alexandre looked at the trio admiringly. He felt like he was going back in time. When, just like them, he was deeply interested in the history of his country. The teacher first took his time finishing a bottle of soda before responding.

"Well, Christophe's motto was *God, My Cause and My Sword.* "

"What was this cause?" interrupted Caroline unceremoniously.

"It was a two-fold cause. First, he wanted to see all Haitians educated. Second, he wanted to buy the Spanish side of Hispaniola to prevent the French from returning and restart the fight for the entire island. He saved a large sum for this purpose. Much of the money was hidden in the fortress of *Citadelle Laferrière*. Unfortunately, many believed that Henry Christophe was taking advantage of the political threat and selfishly hiding money for his family and himself."

A sleuth of questions invaded Ludovic's mind. He thought about the words crest on his drawing: *God and My Cause*. Could this inscription, therefore, be only a shortened form of the king's motto? Was the treasure simply money? Where could have his grandfather hid this money? Unlike Tonton Blain, his half-brother lived almost in poverty.

Caroline also pouted in disappointment. She, too, wondered what was the of use money that is over a century old can be.

"Christophe didn't trust anyone," continued the teacher. "During the building of the *Citadelle*, under the excuse of making sure that everything was going well, he went there night and day. It is believed that in fact he wanted to make sure that the hiding place where he kept his savings would never be discovered."

"But when he died, it was discovered," confidently added Ludovic.

"Oh, no!" the teacher said waving his finger. "The looters took the funds from the national treasury; which means that they only stole the fiscal revenue of the Northern State. But, no one could find the royal treasure. That has raised doubts in the minds of many, that this treasure ever existed."

Caroline shook her head in disapproval. So why did the note written by Queen Marie-Louise said to search tirelessly? Why had Tonton Blain taken such pains to tell them to defend the cause? Why did Mr. Paul leave a family tree to his grandson?

Caroline and Ludovic secretly shouted in their minds: "Yes! The treasure exists, sir! And, we will find it!"

Mr. Alexandre looked at the clock and hastily gathered his things.

"Children, I have to leave. I have another class at 3 p.m."

"Sir," said Ludovic, "one last thing, please. Who are Richard and the officers who looted the *Citadelle*?

"Let's talk about that next Thursday, shall we?"

Next Thursday? Four days to wait!

Ludovic, Caroline, and Eva left the teachers' lounge without saying a word. This cause that Tonton Blain and Mr. Paul told them to defend could not be just a dead-end pursuit, just a simple myth.

"Ludo, are you going home?" Caroline finally asked.

"Yeah."

"Why don't we drop you off? I don't think my dad would mind."

Ludovic was too tired to refuse. He had a defeated look in his eyes and in his body. Caroline shared his emotions. The information they discovered from the teacher blew up all their assumptions. The mirror and the coins that Ludovic treasured until now, could they be the only things that his grandfather wanted to bequeath him? Why would he make him swear not to pass it on to anyone? Maybe François Blain and his brother, who were both from Cap-Haitian, knew of Christophe's motto and had adopted it. He might have bought the paintings somewhere and collected them. No doubt, the Blain brothers had fun creating this mystery for both of their families.

Upon reaching home, Caroline was reminded of the events of the day. She felt that her friendship with Natalie could be ruined if she did not act immediately. In all the years they had known each other, they had never argued before. Yet, in Natalie's shoes, she would have acted no differently. Beside her school choir, nothing mattered expect for Ludovic's paper. She was indeed spending a lot of time with him; also, she could not bear the frivolity of Natalie and the other girls while she had this mystery to uncover.

Thinking about Natalie, brought out Caroline's youthful side. Suddenly, she missed her friend's laughter. She wanted to hear her worthless reflections. She went down to the living room, took a deep breath, then dialed her friend's number.

"Hello."

"Nat? It's me Caro."

"What do you want?"

A chill ran through Caroline's back. She never heard Natalie speaking so harshly.

"I wanted to tell you that there is nothing between Ludovic and I. We are just..."

"Is it only for that you are calling me?! Why are you doing this to me, Caroline?!"

Caroline did not know what to say. She held back her words. Was Natalie that invested in Ludovic? How could she have imagined that she was seriously in love with this one?

Chapter 12

he next day, Natalie relocated herself to one of the rows near the windows. Rumors had it that she was trying to get placed in *Rheto B* – another 11th grade class to finish the school year. She could no longer stand the sight of Caroline anymore. Although hurt by Natalie's attitude, Caroline kept her cool. She was hoping that her friend would come to her senses.

When the anticipated Thursday finally arrived, impatience ate at Caroline and Ludovic all day. Time never seemed to be moving so slowly. Eva could not join them.

At the exact hour of the appointment, they found Mr. Alexandre sitting on a little wall in front of the teachers' lounge. He took a bag full of peppermint candy and offered some to the teenagers.

"What did you want to know again?" he asked them.

"We wanted to know who are Richard and the officers who looted the *Citadelle*, sir?" Ludovic asked while taking some peppermint candies from the bag.

"Well, his complete name was Jean-Pierre Richard. He was the governor of Cap-Henry. At some point, he had the ambitions to overthrow the monarchy and form a republic with him as the president. So, he ended up revolting against the king."

"And what about the officers who were with him?" asked Caroline.

"I never discovered who they were. They were never mentioned on any official manuscripts. However, a name widely retained in popular folk history is that of the Earl of Citronade - King Henry's most faithful ally."

Caroline could not help but smiling upon hearing the name.

"Yeah! There were funny names in the kingdom of Henry 1st."

"Sir, what was the earl's real name?" Ludovic asked.

"That, I don't remember. But according to what they say, he married Claire Twist who was a lady-in-waiting at the *Palais Sans-Souci*."

"Twist?" Caroline wondered. "That's an English name."

"Henry Christophe entertained excellent relationships with England. In the King's court, there were English doctors, teachers, artists and so on. There was an academy of fine arts. Art was at the center of this kingdom."

Suddenly, Ludovic remembered he tried to reproduce the drawing during Physiology class. He took his notebook out of his bag and showed the picture to the teacher.

"Sir, did Henry Christophe by chance commissioned a drawing of the legs of an animal that looked like these?"

Mr. Alexandre frowned and took the sheet from Ludovic's hands.

"Yes. Christophe's coat of arms consisted of two lions."

Caroline jumped with happiness.

"Well, Miss Lebrun, there's more than lion's paws in the coat of arms. Too bad I am not an artist like you Mr. Paul…"

Mr. Alexandre examined the drawing a little closer by lifting his glasses.

"However, I have the impression that what you drew here may be a heraldry."

"A heraldry?" asked Ludovic puzzled.

"There were important families attached to the reign of Henry Christophe. They also had their own coat of arms. And that may be what this drawing represents. Take a good look. The ribbon doesn't say *God, My Cause and My Sword"* like that of the king. But *God and My Cause.* This was the motto of the Espérance family."

Four pairs of bulging eyes zoomed on the teacher.

"Anyway, next year, all this information will be part of your curriculum. You will be able to delve deeply into the information, as you wish," said Mr. Alexandre while returning the drawing.

"One moment, sir. Did you say Espérance Family?" Ludovic asked with a shortened breath.

"Yes. It was one of the important families of Cap-Henry, as well as the Simons, the Twists and so on."

Caroline's heart leapt out of her chest. Ludovic's blood froze in his veins. If time was crawling all day long for the pair, now it just simply stopped. Mr. Alexandre did not realize how valuable of an information he just revealed.

Chapter 13

ext week, we will review the effects of sending the Second Civil Commission to Saint Domingue. Have a good day class."

Rapidly, Mr. Alexandre picked up the homework that the students placed on his desk. With a gesture, he asked Caroline and Ludovic to join him. As the rest of the class was leaving for recess, they rushed toward the teacher.

Mr. Alexandre pulled a big book out of his bag. The pages were a little yellowed and torn in places.

"I think this might be of interest to you children."

Caroline's heart was pounding as she waited for Mr. Alexandre to open the book to a pre-selected page. He produced a photocopy of a picture.

"This is what the king's coat of arms looks like."

The teenagers stared at two lions standing on their hind legs and each had a golden crown on their head. With their front paws, they held a banner on which was written: *Je renais de mes cendres* – From my ashes I am reborn. Above a flag, there a representation of a crowned bird; the crown was identical to the lions' crown. A chain made up of lockets went around it while a star-shaped pendant clung to it. The lions were standing on a ribbon, on which was written in French in golden letters the words: *Dieu, Ma Cause et Mon Épée* – God, My Cause and My Sword.

Caroline hugged the teacher. Caught off guard by this spontaneous expression of joy, Mr. Alexandre let out a smile.

"Now, look at the heraldry of the Espérances."

The teacher took the copy and handed it to Caroline and Ludovic. The drawing was almost the same as that of the king's coat of arms. Except that instead of two lions, there was a lion and a horse and the banner read: *Dieu et Ma Cause* - God and My Cause.

Ludovic and Caroline could not believe that they were finally looking at the drawing they had been searching for so long.

"You can keep it," the teacher told them.

"Thank you, sir!"

"Go on, now! I will see you Monday. Don't let your next summer vacation derail your studies. The final school exam, the *Bacc Blanc* (mock Bacc exam) and the official

Department of Education exam are right around the corner. Put all your effort into and prepare well," concluded Mr. Alexandre without allowing Caroline and her friend to ask any more questions.

Once the teacher left, Caroline and Ludovic jumped in each other's arms. So many months of research were now bearing fruit. Both ran out of their classroom ready to shout their happiness. They were so eager to tell Eva everything.

Ludovic and Caroline found Eva on the courtyard. She was chatting with some classmates. Seeing her jumping cousin, Eva understood that some exiting news awaited her. The trio went to the library and find a spot to discuss.

"Man!" Eva blurted out when she saw the drawing.

"Maybe, the Simon family and the others in the family tree also have their heraldry," said Ludovic proudly.

"Did you ask Redingote?"

"Nope. We didn't have time."

"Well, should I now call you Sir Ludovic?" asked Eva.

The question caused a burst of laughter. The librarian looked in their direction and asked them to be quiet by putting her finger in front of her mouth.

"Shhh," Eva said mockingly.

"So, let's recap" suggested Caroline in a low voice. "Marie-Louise Christophe leaves us a message telling us to defend the cause…"

"That's number one," said Eva.

"For the second step," continued Caroline, "the novel tells us about Ludovic's list."

"But it also speaks of sculpted objects," added her cousin.

"My mirror," said Ludovic.

"Without a doubt. But the word "objects" is in plural," pointed out Caroline.

The trio paused for a moment. Unlike Ludovic's mirror, the Lebruns' paintings were not sculpted objects.

"All the other sculpted art we have at home is from artists my parents know."

"So, we haven't found anything yet," concluded Ludovic.

Leaning on the table, Caroline supported her head with both hands. This whole story was driving her crazy.

Chapter 14

r. Alexandre was right. The dates for the *Bac Blanc* exams were coming. The principal was now on a full campaign of sensibilizing the students to do their best. A month and a half before the official exams, she wanted them to understand the importance of these tests to themselves and the school. She stressed the school's tradition of success among the best in the capital and obtaining the highest scores at the Baccalaureate.

Caroline's parents were happy to see their daughter as well as Eva and Ludovic spending hours and hours under the pergola reviewing chemistry, physics, and math courses and they did so even on the weekends. Each one leaned on the other for their strength and weakness in some subjects. Sometimes, a few Eva's classmates were invited. Those time turned the courtyard into a mobile classroom. Often their meetings ended with a sort of small party where appetizers and soft drinks were served until early evening.

After the *Bac Blanc* series of exams, the principal entered Caroline's Spanish class. Her presence raised everyone's stress.

"Hello Mr. Garcia. Hello Class," she said.

As one body, the students rose and unanimously returned with an "Hello" of their own.

"Thank you, children. You may sit down."

Caroline and the whole class had their eyes now glued on the folder the principal was holding.

"I just personally wanted to congratulate this class for the results it scored in the *Bac Blanc*. I don't have to tell any of you here that the exams were very difficult. We were quite aware of that, but you all can be proud! None of you failed. We believe that you are now well prepared for the real exams which official dates are rapidly approaching. Again congratulations!"

The whole class started to applaud and Caroline even more. She let out a sigh of relief. She was so afraid that she had failed several tests. But failing was the last thing she wanted. Caroline knew that having her own cell phone depended on her performance on the official exams.

"However," continued the principal, "this is not the end of the journey. You have little time left before the official exams in July. This will be the time to hone your skills and work on your weaknesses."

While speaking, the principal opened the folder she was holding and took out a sheet which she stuck to her chest.

"In the meantime, as you all know, we have a custom here at Audubon School. After the *Bac Blanc*, the 20 students from *Rheto* and *Philo* – 11th and 12 grade - who obtain 1200 points and more out of a total of 1400 points, will go with us on a field trip in one of the country's major cities."

Caroline's heartbeat quickened. Last year, Eva missed it by a few points. She had had so much trouble mastering chemistry formulas. She still can remember Ludovic's patiently explaining to her again and again all the tricks to use to solve certain mathematical equations. Even in language and in historical essay, she was certain that she had not done her best. Caroline therefore barely listened; happy in advance for all those who would be selected.

"Last year," said the principal, "we went in the South-East in Jacmel. This year, we will go to the North. The city is the second most important city in the country: Cap-Haitian."

Caroline's stamped her feet while Ludovic at the back of the class let out a "Yes!" which surprised everybody.

With one hand behind his back, the Spanish teacher standing near the principal, was amused by Ludovic's and Caroline's reaction. From where she sat, Caroline at times, turned in Natalie's direction. But her classmate was keeping her head straight and seemed to be waiting only for the moment when her own name would be mentioned.

"Well," said the principal, "remember that all of you will not have the chance to go. So, here are the names."

The names were not in alphabetical order. The list was according to the scores obtained from lowest to highest. To make the suspense last, the principal took her time to reveal each name. The emotion was palpable. While some names were a surprise, others were not. Caroline felt her temperature rise. From time to time, she turned back to look at Ludovic. His complexion was turning orange, his laughing eyes were getting brighter as his stress was going higher.

"With a score of 1239 points, we have Anne Caroline Lebrun."

Caroline let out a cry of joy. She could not believe it. Finally, she was going to the city where Marie-Louis Coidavid was born, where she grew up, and where she became a queen. Finally, she was going to be able to see with her own eyes the landscape depicted in the picture. Finally, she was going to walk on the ruins of the *Palais Sans-Souci.* Maybe, she would be able to find a clue that would allow her to solve the enigma that Tonton Blain left them with. And maybe, who knows, they would stay at the *Hotel de la Couronne.* The suspense was high now. Was Ludovic as lucky as her? And how about Eva? Would she also be selected this time?

The principal revealed even slowly the names of each selected student because she realized the excitement her list was causing. She decided to say a few words about each result.

"Finally, we have Ludovic Xavier Paul with 1300 points!"

The whole class applauded. Thanks to his scores in sciences, Ludovic was among the three students who had obtained the highest scores in the class.

The final bell rang and this could not have come at a better time. Caroline and Ludovic needed to shout their joy without restrictions. Once the principal and the teacher left, they quickly packed up their bags and left the classroom. They hugged each other in the hallway. Natalie was looking at them. Caroline saw her sadness mixed with a certain anger that she had never noticed in her before. Natalie missed the chance by five points.

Eva also came out of her class running toward Ludovic and her cousin.

"I am going to Cap-Haitian!" she cried out.

"WE are going to Cap-Haitian!" Caroline corrected.

"Ahhhhh!" the two cousins cried out at the same time.

They were holding hands while jumping with joy. Ludovic took his cap out of his bag and put it on his head before picking up a sheet from the floor that Caroline had dropped. It was the instructions that those who were selected had to follow. Caroline compared it with Eva's.

"It says the same things," noticed her cousin.

"I wonder why do the girls have to bring a long skirt and a matching upper and the boys cloth pants and a long-sleeved shirt?" wondered Caroline out of breath.

"It says it's for an 'Unforgettable Evening'. Maybe we'll have a dance party." indicated Eva.

Caroline made a face.

"No way I'm dancing with the guys in my class."

"Won't you dance with me?" asked Ludovic with one outstretched arm and the other on his heart.

"Ah!" cried Caroline. "No way you're stepping on my delicate feet!"

Caroline's father beeped his horn to get their attention because he was parked across the street.

"Are you taking a ride with us today too?" Eva asked Ludovic.

The young main accepted. He rushed into the street to stop traffic and allow the two cousins to cross. A group of students who were waiting for an opportunity to do the same, crossed with them. Eva got into the front of the car, while Caroline and Ludovic rushed into the back.

"Hi, dad. Ludo is riding with us today."

Caroline took her dad off guard and left him no possibility to refuse.

"OK," said Mr. Lebrun slowly. "I do have to go somewhere though. I hope you don't have to be home right away, Ludovic?"

"No sir."

"Dad, guess what?"

"What?"

"All three of us were selected to go to a field trip in Cap-Haitian next week!"

Caroline's father looked at his daughter through the rear-view mirror. The school had already informed the parents of the selected students in advance to better prepare for the trip. But all parents were instructed not to reveal anything to their kids. Caroline's parents therefore played the game to the point that the teenage girl believed she was the first to break the news.

"Congratulations, children! I am very proud of you! That's what hard work brings. On the other hand, the official exams will be for next month. You all should not forget that."

Caroline was certainly not going to forget. She wanted that cell phone too much. She had even already chosen the model and color she wanted. As soon as they got back from their trip and their research was done, she and the others would go back to revising.

Mr. Lebrun was driving a little faster than usual. The children were being knocked around in the back. Ludovic's bag opened and spilled his books on his lap. Caroline recognized the sketchbook he always had with him.

"What are you drawing this week? She asked while putting some toasted peanuts in her mouth.

Ludovic opened the sketchbook and showed his drawing.

"A pair of shoes."

"Wow! You would think it's a photo!" admired Caroline.

"Let me see," said Eva from the front.

"Ludovic is a real artist," quickly said Caroline.

"Where did you…," Mr. Lebrun started to say. But a colorful *Tap Tap* (a minibus taxi) nearly hit the front of his car. He honked loudly several times before turning right to let the bus pass.

"Ruffians," he shouted.

Both hands on the wheel, Caroline's father deftly took a little-known back road to get ahead of the traffic jam, and get to his appointment on time.

"What did you mean earlier?" Caroline resumed once she felt that her father had calmed down a bit.

"About what?" he asked a little lost.

"What were you about to ask?"

"Oh yes! I wanted to know where did Ludovic learn to draw like this."

"I take classes at the *Centre d'Art*," replied the young man.

"The *Centre d'Art*? I thought it was just an art gallery."

"Yes. But for a very long time every Saturday a well-known artist gives lessons in the gardens."

Mr. Lebrun nodded. Caroline wanted to say something, but she held back. Her father's gaze met hers in the rearview mirror. She squeezed her lips and turned her head sideways. What is the point of talking about what she would like. She had an already-made path designed by her father and mother: after graduating from high school, she will go straight to law school.

Her father understood her silence and smiled.

"Would you like to attend that course, Caro?" he finally asked.

Astonished, Caroline turned her head towards the rear-view mirror.

"Yes," she replied forcefully, without a moment of hesitation.

"Then you will go during the summer vacations."

Caroline grabbed Ludovic's hand. Today was the day of all surprises.

Chapter 15

uickly, the school's weekend trip arrived. The day before, with the help of her mother, Caroline and her cousin spent hours making sure they were taking what they needed and the requested items on the school list. Caroline's mother looked with amusement the comings and goings of the two teenage girls.

"Take this bag instead. And don't forget to take also your raincoat and this first aid kit."

"Mom, I'm sure the principal will be planning for all kind of things. I just want to bring my backpack."

Caroline carefully packed in her bag some underwear, two tops, a shirt, a long skirt, and a pair of sneakers. She wanted to add also her sketchbook, her colored pencils, and her new camera. But she realized that her mother might have been right. She needed a bigger bag. She and her cousin were going a long trip. Any small emergencies can become a nightmare. To her mother's great relief, Caroline accepted the bigger bag and made good use of it.

"Anyway, I am sure the principal isn't planning to have any make-up sets for us. So, I am taking mine!" said Eva.

Caroline burst out laughing. Of course, her cousin went ahead with packing a large make-up set, a few lip-glosses of different shades, her hair iron, several fancy dresses, two small handbags, ballet flats, pumps, heeled sandals, and whatever else she could squeeze in her carry-on.

"This suitcase might become dangerous. The bus might be too heavy and crash under all this weight!" Caroline pointed out.

On the day of departure, it was a bit difficult to recognize anybody at first glance. The gray jersey stamped with the initials of Audubon School was obligatory for everyone during the entire trip. The principal in jeans, cell phone in hand, was helped by her assistants, Mr. Alexandre and three other teachers.

At 7 a.m. sharp, the bus driver's assistant closed the luggage compartment and got into the vehicle. The bus headed to the heart of downtown. At this hour, the traffic was a little fluid and the other drivers were visibly afraid of this large vehicle. Soon the driver was at the *Bicentenaire* and took the *Route Nationale #1* which would lead them straight to Cap-Haitian.

The principal and Mr. Alexandre were already in a deep conversation. Unlike the trip to *Fort-Jacques*, Caroline, Eva and Ludovic were seated a bit too far from the teacher. They were looking to talk to him whenever the opportunities would present themselves. So, they went over all the questions they wanted answers to.

Caroline copied her letter and the message of the novel onto her sketchbook. Ludovic brought a copy of his paper and the drawing of the heraldry of the Espérances.

"Do you think that you will be able to track your grandfather's family there?" Eva asked Ludovic.

"Not sure. My mom doesn't have a phone number and she's only been to Cap-Haitian once in her lifetime."

"No worries. We will eventually find the answers to our questions," reassured Caroline.

This trip was quite different and more comfortable than the trip to *Fort-Jacques*. The bus was air-conditioned and more mechanically sound. They could barely feel the bus going over the many potholes on the road. They were at ease on the padded chair. Ludovic took advantage of all of it. He had his arms and legs on two seats feeling like a king. Caroline burst out laughing when she saw him.

"I hope you paid for both," said Eva.

"At least the coming long hours won't feel like martyrdom, "said Caroline.

"Oh Lord!" Eva suddenly wondered. "I completely forgot about *Puilboreau* mountain! I wish we were able to fly instead of the bus."

Caroline nodded. Her cousin was right. The trip would have been shorter, just thirty minutes in the air. It would have saved them more than six hours on the road.

"I don't think my parents would have accepted that we go. It would be way too expensive," Caroline admitted after reflection.

"Nay! *Puilboreau* mountain is nothing, I assure you. It's not scary at all," Ludovic blurted out.

"Really?" Caroline asked while giving him a sideways look. "How do you know? When did you first experience the mountain?"

Ludovic scratched his chin.

"Uh... When I was three or four years old."

Caroline and Eva burst out laughing. Mr. Alexandre who was going to the back of the bus, suddenly stopped near them. They were startled.

"I have never seen students so happy to visit Cap-Haitian. Will you all go with your parents again during the summer?"

Caroline had a moment of hesitation before answering. Caught off guard, she forgot that it was the excuse she and her cousin gave him to quell his curiosity and stop any suspicion.

"Since we are going now, my parents decided to do something else."

"Ah, ok," said the teacher before joining a colleague in the back.

Music was coming from loudspeakers. A few students in the back recognized the tune playing on the radio. Those in the middle started to sing parts of the lyrics while others sang the chorus. Soon everyone joined in and the whole bus was now a karaoke bus.

The vehicle continued carefully on the road. The travelers got a glimpse of the *Cote des Arcadins* and its miles of white sand beaches. From the start, one assistant who took the trouble to keep them informed on each town they passed through, announced that they were in *Saint-Marc*. Caroline was not really paying attention. Having traveled on this highway so often with her parents, she knew all the beaches in the area. Ludovic took from his backpack some cards and asked the girls who wanted to play with him. Eva volunteered first. Caroline was finishing a drawing.

"Children!" said Mr. Alexandre. "We are now in the *department* of *Artibonite*. Who can tell us some cultural or historical facts related to this area?"

Caroline looked up.

"It is the largest rice producer," she answered.

"Very good! Indeed, in terms of rice production, this *department* is the most conducive to rice cultivation because of the *Artibonite* River. It is also the longest river in the country… Anything else?"

Caroline and a few other students were scratching their heads for a few moments but Ludovic had a quick answer.

"This is the *department* where Jean-Jacques Dessalines declared our independence from France in 1804."

"This is where the capital of the country once was," said another student.

"People in the area like to eat *lalo*," said his companion.

"Bravo!" praised the teacher.

Mr. Alexandre paused and waited for other responses. He decided to break the prolonged silence.

"It's in this *department*, precisely in the area of *Petite-Rivière de l'Artibonite* that the *Palais de la Belle Rivière* is located. I am sure you have heard of that Palace."

Caroline and her classmates did not seem to know what the teacher was referring to.

"You know this palace, kids. It's the one that is wrongly called the *Palais aux 365 portes* – The 365 doors Palace. Its construction began in 1820, under the reign of Henry Christophe.

Caroline, Eva, and Ludovic straightened up in their seats at the same time, as if an order was given to them. The principal took an envelope and took out a stack of papers. Each student received a copy.

There was a photo of the Palace on the sheet with its official name and exact location. Eva and Ludovic stopped playing cards. Eva returned to her seat. Caroline closed her sketchbook and wiped her fingers clean. She then quickly rummaged through her backpack and found a pen.

"As you can see on the sheet, this palace was to serve as a secondary residence for King Henry 1st."

"What was the main residence, sir?" Ludovic asked.

"The *Palais Sans-Souci* that we will visit in Milot."

The teenagers were beyond happy. The *Palais Sans-Souci* was the palace displayed in the painting in Caroline's living room.

"We are here in the vast and rich agricultural region of the *Artibonite* which in the 1800s marked the limits of the Kingdom of Henry Christophe," continued Mr. Alexandre.

"It was at the limit of this department that the Republic of Pétion began," added the principal.

"Exactly, ma'am."

Caroline, who was taking notes relentlessly, stopped and raised her finger.

"Sir, why did you say that it was wrongly called *Palais aux 365 portes* ?"

"It's precisely because the palace doesn't have 365 doors. It has many openings that give this illusion. But the architecture was thus planned to allow the air to circulate better, especially during summer."

The bus arrived at the city of *Gonaïves*. The passengers would be able to stretch their legs and use the restrooms. Before stepping out, the principal reminded the students of the does and don'ts of the trip. Street vendors besieged the bus with sugar cane, sweet potato pies and chips, plantain chips, corn bread, and drinks. All the students rushed to stock up. Eva chose her absolute favorites of *bonbon siwo* - gingerbread- and some puff mints.

After a controlled pandemonium brought on by the sweets, the bus occupants fell gradually silent. The fatigue of the journey was beginning to take its toll and any laughter became more and more sporadic. Eva was the first to doze off. Ludovic, who was playing solitaire, ended up closing his eyes. Caroline was the only one waiting for the famous *Puilboreau* mountain.

To pass the time, she opened her notebook and started another drawing. She imagined what the Simon and the Twist heraldry might look like. At times she would have liked to ask Mr. Alexandre for some guidance. But like everybody else, he was sleeping. Only the principal seemed to have the same energy as her. The principal was deeply invested in some scheme. From time to time, she wrote something in a notebook or talked to the driver and his assistant or looked for something in her cell phone. Caroline noticed the device in her hands. It was exactly the model and color she wanted. It was small enough to be housed in her bag or her pocket.

As soon as the driver told his assistant not to make the announcement, Caroline knew that the bus just left the town called *Ennery* and was beginning the climbing of the more than two thousand feet high *Puilboreau* mountain. Houses disappeared. The winding road offered on each side the view of lush vegetation. Small potholes in the middle of the road rocked the bus a little. To give more power to the engine, the driver turned off the air conditioning, rolled down the windows and changed gears more than once. This maneuver woke up some of the sleeping passengers.

"We are climbing," said Caroline softly to her cousin.

"What?" replied Eva, a little dazed by sleep.

"We are on the *Puilboreau* mountain."

Eva sat up a little worried. She looked out the window. She closed her eyes hastily. The road was narrow and each motorcycle, private car or another bus was appearing like a dangerous surprise in the sharp curves. With the altitude Eva's heartbeat quickened. She opened a bottle of water and took a sip.

Ludovic asked Caroline to join him. On his side, the view was quite different. Beside the cliff, the path traveled could be seen below. The roofs of a few scattered houses appeared in the lush valley at the foot of several mountain ranges that rose in the distance under a cloudless sky. Caroline adjusted her camera and took some pictures. She then closed her eyes and offered her face to the pure air that rushed into the bus.

"If only you could see this!" she said excitely to her cousin.

"No!" replied Eva with a hand in front of her eyes. "It's sickening!"

Usually, Eva was very adventurous. But this mountain made her so pressured that she could burst into tears. Caroline went back to sit next to Ludovic. She did not want to miss the down-hill descent towards Cap-Haitian. Indeed, it was said that once you reach the summit, the road follows a beautiful serpentine line. She and Ludovic kept passing the camera to each other to capture the shots of a lifetime.

The bus finally reached the valley at the foot of the mountain. The experience of the high altitude worn out the strength and put a stress on everyone's body. Eva had a migraine. Ludovic now could barely keep his eyes opened. Only Caroline kept on taking pictures. She was the only one ready for the adventure.

Chapter 16

hildren, welcome to Cap-Haitian!" said proudly Mr. Alexandre.

With this announcement, the students sat up straight in their seats. They turned their heads from right to left to see the city fully. The previous silence gave way to whispers and the sounds of backpacks closing. Brightly colored colonial-era houses stood proudly on the narrow streets. Caroline took pictures of these houses with wrought ironed balconies that seemed to have seen history passing below on the streets.

Although they were used to seeing thousands of tourists, the bus aroused the curiosity of many locals. Some children were eating *ti Carol* – ice cream in a bag - in front of a shop. They energetically greeted them. Women carrying various items on their heads and slowly laboring under their burdens took their time to watch the new comers. Soon, the bus entered through the gates of a hotel. Ludovic looked at his watch. It was 2 pm.

"Are you ok, Eva?" asked Caroline.

Eva was looking haggard. She shook her head. Her migraine was getting worst. Caroline opened her bag and gave her a bottle of water and one of the painkillers her mother packed in the first aid kit.

The principal and her assistant came down first and headed for the hotel reception while the teachers and the students were taking their luggage under the bus. Ludovic helped Eva drag hers as she leaned on Caroline's arm.

"Man, Eva!" said Ludovic. "Do you have a dead body in there or something?"

Caroline just smiled. She knew that half her cousin's wardrobe was in there.

Auberge Laferrière was at the end of a brick alley lined with bright pink bougainvillea. It was quite frequented by many tourists and foreign university students. A few days earlier such a group arrived and they were lounging on the large and long porch that almost encircled the building. Caroline noticed the foreign students as she and other students were crossing the porch to join the principal in the hotel's lobby. A glass of fruit juice with a slice of pineapple greeted them.

Throughout the property, there were palm trees and ferns that enhanced the beauty of the mahogany furniture. Caroline looked up and examined the ceiling beams that stood exposed against the curvature of the roof and the off-white the walls showcasing dozens of paintings by local artists.

The students were put in groups of two before receiving the key to their room. They were to meet in an hour and a half in the dining room. A small inner courtyard connected the front of the hotel to the rooms at the back. They followed the hotel staff who led them to a suite of rooms built outside the main building in the middle of a lush garden.

Caroline opened her bedroom door followed by her cousin. Eva walked straight to one of the two beds and collapsed on it. The room was not luxurious but neat. A lamp was on the bedside table that separated the two beds while another sat on a desk placed close to the only window in the room. It was quite a large window. Caroline parted the curtains and was surprise that the window overlooked the garden that surrounded the property. She closed the curtains and put her backpack on the desk. Above, a brightly colored painting of the *Citadelle Laferrière* caught her eyes. The style reminded her of a painting that her parents bought a few years earlier from a Cap-Haitian painter.

Caroline took off her shoes and went to the bathroom. As she passed by her cousin, she saw her in a deep sleep. Caroline felt a bit of anxiety. What would she do if Eva was really sick? She was so far from the capital, so far from her parents. This dream weekend was to be the most beautiful of the year. How was she going to be able to do the research and at the same time take care of Eva?

The bathroom was modern and spacious. Caroline quickly took her bath, put on a clean t-shirt, her jeans and sneakers, and left the room. She soon realized that she was the first to be ready for dinner. But she did not want to go back to her room. She was not tired. She did not want to watch Eva sleep. She decided to explore the place instead. After all, she was in the Queen's city and every step on this land was in itself filled with history.

The teenage girl walked alone in the garden surrounding the hotel. A few banana trees, treated as ornamental plants, were already booming among parsley erected stone sculptures. Caroline stopped and took some pictures. In the inner courtyard, a few water lilies planted in a pond attracted dragonflies. Caroline bent down to play in the water with the insects. She then got up to admire a set of plants arranged in clay pots of astonishing shapes. She continued her visit and without knowing how, she found herself at the front of the hotel. The foreigners were still on the porch, swinging on rocking chairs while chatting. They were architecture students from a university in Ottawa. They were traveling the Caribbean as part of a project on post-colonial architecture. Haiti was their last destination before returning home. Caroline could not help but listening to them. She did not fully understand what they were saying. Yet she heard enough to realized that they were still marveling at their visit of the *Citadelle.*

"Hello!" said a young woman from the group who had noticed her.

Caroline looked around her. Nobody was there. The terribly tanned girl had indeed greeted her. Caroline took a deep breath. Five years of English at school and all those summer vacations in New York, surely prepared her for a simple conversation in that foreign language. But it is at first in a timid voice that she replied:

"Hello! "

The whole group turned to Caroline. They all had that tanned complexion, proof of a beach getaway.

"Where are you from?" continued Caroline.

"Canada," replied the girl. "Are you from here?"

"No. I am from Port-au-Prince. I am visiting with my school."

"We went to the *Citadelle* this morning!" informed the girl.

"Of my God!" interrupted a young man of the same age. "What a magnificent place!"

"I am pretty sure you've been there many times!"

The English words were coming a little too fast for Caroline's ears. But she managed to understand that the visitors were amazed by the architecture of the *Citadelle*. Though she has not visited it yet, she remembered what Mr. Alexandre told them during their excursion to *Fort-Jacques* and the stories of Tonton Blain.

One of the boys got up and left his rocking chair for Caroline. The enthusiasm of the students was contagious. Caroline threw herself into a lively discussion punctuated by laughter though understanding partially. She became even more confident when she realized that she was understood even when with her *Frenglish*.

"Miss Lebrun, what are you doing here by yourself?"

Caroline jumped. Mr. Alexandre was standing behind her with a worried face. Suddenly the teenage girl realized that her teacher has been searching for her.

"Sorry, sir. They are students from Ottawa and they wanted to know a lot about our history."

The teacher chatted a bit with the group in perfect English. Astonished, Caroline looked at him with admiration. She never knew he spoke English. She was even prouder of her teacher as he answered all their questions to satisfaction.

"We must go, now," said finally Mr. Alexandre. "The others are already in the dining room."

The group of foreign students thanked Caroline who left alongside the teacher.

"Miss Lebrun, remember that we must all stay together at all times."

"I'm sorry, sir. I just wanted to explore the place."

"It doesn't matter now… And where is your cousin?"

Caroline completely forgot about Eva.

"She is still in the room. She has a big headache."

"Did you inform the principal?"

"Uh, no… But she took some pills and she is resting."

Mr. Alexandre walked through the inner courtyard close to the lobby. Instead of taking the path that led to the bedrooms, he turned to the right in the direction of the dining room.

"Let's take a shortcut. The restaurant is on this side."

"Sir, are we going to visit the *Hôtel de la Couronne*?"

The teacher smiled.

"No. We won't have time. But, don't worry. We have a full program. I'm sure you will like it. In the meantime, go eat with your friends."

When Caroline and Mr. Alexandre arrived in the dining room, the principal was standing near the buffet and her assistant was making sure that all the students were served. The teacher walked toward her and let her know that a student was not well. Immediately, she gave her assistant the plates she was holding and headed toward Eva and Caroline's bedroom.

The dining room was at the rear of the hotel and went all the way to a partly covered terrace. Almost at the end of the terrace, several tables were placed side by side to allow the students to stay together. Not far from there, there were the teachers' table. Ludovic and a few other students in their class waved at Caroline's.

"Where were you?" asked Ludovic.

Caroline took a moment before answering. She was captivated by the view in front of her. The terrace opened to the sea in the distance. The sun was about to set. The sight simply took Caroline's breath away.

"Long story," she finally answered. "What are we eating?"

"You better go and see yourself," replied one of the students. "There is almost nothing left."

"I imagine you swallowed it all," joked Caroline.

Ludovic's plate had a little bit of everything in it. But one dish in particular caught Caroline's attention.

"What is that?"

"A specialty from the North: *Poulets au Noix* (Chicken with Walnuts)," Ludovic replied before eating the delicious piece of meat.

"And it's good?"

"Very, very good. It's even better than my mom's recipe."

Caroline left Ludovic and went to the buffet. A waiter started to bring out a variety of plates from the kitchen. Caroline looked for something she never tasted before.

"Could I have some chicken with walnut?"

"Sure," answered the waiter. "And you want what type of rice with it?"

There were several kinds of rice. But the perfectly white one smelled good.

"White rice, please."

"I would suggest that you add a little bit of green beans puree with it," said the waiter.

"Ok."

Caroline put only a small portion of the dish on her plate. She wanted to try it by itself and not let any other food alter the taste. While heading to the students' table, she met Ludovic who was going for a second round at the buffet.

From the first bite, the delicious taste of the chicken surprised Caroline's taste buds. The more she ate, the more she wanted to eat. Caroline was thinking about her cousin. She offered to make a plat for her and bring it to the room. But Eva was there. She was coming with Ludovic.

"Eva!" Caroline exclaimed pulling out the chair next to her. "How are you feeling?"

"Better. The migraine is gone."

Each student took different dishes they wanted but all were eating with appetite the chicken with walnuts.

"What are you guys eating like that?" Eva asked.

"I am not going to tell you. You must taste it yourself! It's so good!" said Caroline enthusiastically.

"I told you, didn't I?" added Ludovic.

In a corner on the terrace, five musicians were setting up. Caroline got up and turned her chair a little so that she could see and hear them better. Ludovic, Eva and, a few other students did the same. Soon, the banjo players started singing along with the one who was shaking his cha-cha.

"What is this man playing?" Caroline asked, pointing to one of the band members sitting behind the other musicians.

"It's a kind of drum," answered Ludovic.

The musician was indeed playing on what seemed to be a box with a round hole where iron blades came out. He fingered the blades while banging on the crate he was sitting on. The music was catchy. Many of the hotel guests were unable to resist any longer. They got up and started to dance.

The mixture of troubadour and *konpa* music opened the improvised ball with a whole repertoire of Haitian folk songs. From their table the teachers and the principal also could not stay still. The lively sounds of the cha-cha, the banjos, and drums were irresistible.

Chapter 17

The next day, the students did not need to be woken up early. Everyone already had their breakfast and were ready for the day. Caroline was the very first among the students to wake up. The stories of the young Canadian enflamed her imagination and expectations.

Caroline made sure she had in her backpack her cap, bottles of water, sketchbook, pencil case, and her first aid kit. Then she put the camera around her neck. Slowly, the students trickled out of their rooms.

"No, miss," said the principal to a student who was boarding the bus. "Go change your shoes. You need to have your sneakers on. We are going to walk a lot today."

Caroline's impatience and lack of sympathy showed on her face. The instructions were clear. What could have made her classmate think she could wear sandals? And now they are wasting time waiting for her to change. Finally, the students came back and the bus took off.

Although the streets were filled with colorful *tap-taps* - the local public transportation vehicles - motorcycles, and bicycles, the traffic in Cap-Haitian was significantly less dense than that of Port-au-Prince's.

"Hello children," said Mr. Alexandre on the microphone.

"Hello, Mr. Alexandre," answered all the students.

"Are you all rested?"

"Yes!"

"Are you all ready?"

"Yes!"

"On the program today, we will first drive around the city a bit to see the architecture. Because after all, that too is history."

"Redingote is super lively this morning," Eva whispered in her cousin's ear.

Caroline nodded. She too thought the same thing. The teacher was in his element. He was happier than usual. His voice was stronger and the tone more playful. Caroline even overheard him during breakfast talking to a hotel staff in the typical northern accent. Caroline understood nothing of the conversation, but the vocabulary amused her.

"As you can tell kids. Cap-Haitian is one of the oldest cities in the country and still retains its old charm. But, when I say old, I am talking old of about 1840. Cap-Haitian was destroyed twice by earthquakes. Once in May 1842 and then in February 1843."

Caroline's mind went straight to the painting of the queen hanging on her living room. She understood now every facial expression in the picture. She now realized that in addition to suffering from her exile, Marie-Louise Coidavid Christophe may have certainly heard about those earthquakes that shook her city. Maybe she was worried about her loved ones back home. Perhaps this news weighed on her heart.

"This city is also the birthplace of many famous Haitian writers. Who can name one of our most famous poets who was born in this city?" asked Mr. Alexandre.

Caroline raised her hand instinctively. She knew all too well the answer.

"Oswald Durand!"

"Exactly! Oswald Durand is the most known Haitian author in the world because of his poem entitled..."

"*Choucoune* !" answered all the students.

The streets were laid at right angles. A narrow street forced the bus to slow down in front of a vividly painted house. A lady, wanting to keep her privacy, closed the door size *jalousie* on her balcony. Caroline hastened to immortalize the scene in a photo. A little further, the two-story houses lined the street in a fanfare explosion of beauty and colors. They were adorned with wrought irons balconies which ran the length of their facade.

Caroline who could not help taking pictures suddenly stopped.

"Sir, are the numbers we are seeing the real names of the streets?"

"Very observant Miss Lebrun. Yes, they are. The streets are numbered and 'alphabetized'."

The students looked puzzled.

"Well, yes. It's a system that combines both number and letters. First, we have the numbers, 1, 2, 3 etc. which point to one direction and then we have the letters of the alphabet which point to the other direction: A B, C, D, etc. So now, we are exactly at the corner of street 15-J. Obviously, the Cap also has streets that have names just like the ones in Port-au-Prince."

While the teacher explained more about the layout of the town, the bus left the heart of the city. It crossed a city gate called *Barrière Bouteille* and headed south toward the town of Milot. Caroline opened her notebook to check the notes she took the day before. Mr. Alexandre then gave them a brief history of that gate that dated back to the colony.

"Children, we are approaching the National Historical Park. This park is made up of the *Citadelle Laferrière, Palais Sans-Souci* and the *Ramiers* site. Since 1982 the whole park has been listed as part of UNESCO World Heritage."

"What is UNESCO World Heritage?" Eva wondered out loud.

"All over the world, there are cultural and natural assets which are unique and specific to a region. Many of these sites have survived time. Their exceptional historical value allows them to be not only the heritage of a nation but also the heritage of the whole humanity. And this is the case of our National Historical Park. It belongs to both Haitians and the people of the world."

The bus finally arrived in the village of Milot. From where he sat, Ludovic was the first to see the outline of a ruined castle. Quickly, he pointed it out to Caroline.

"Look at that!"

"Wow!"

Now that the trip was starting to get very interesting, the bus's microphone was failing Mr. Alexandre. He put it away and continued out loud.

"We will soon pass in front of the ruins of the *Palais Sans-Souci*. We will come back to visit it later. But first, our excursion will start with the visit of the *Citadelle.*"

"Why is that sir?" Caroline asked disappointed.

"Because right this moment we will need all our strength."

Ludovic wanted to see the *Citadelle* at all costs. But Eva and Caroline had no choice but to wait before stepping foot into what really was at the center of their interest: the house where the queen lived. The Canadian students tried to describe the allure of the *Citadelle* to Caroline and she has seen it many times in pictures. But the *Citadelle* was nothing but a fort to her, just like *Fort-Jacques*. Caroline did not care much about past wars. Love stories were what she preferred.

The bus was now climbing a hill.

"Children, get ready to live a weekend like you could never have imagined! We are now on the mountain range called *Bonnet à l'Évêque*. We are going to climb the *Pic Laferrière* until we reach almost 3000 feet high. The bus will not be able to take us to the top. At some point we will have to walk and some may also ride horses."

Eva immediately covered her face with her hands.

"Good God! We are going to climb a 3000-feet mountain!"

"That's not what he said," corrected Caroline in a low voice.

"Don't worry," reassured Ludovic. "I'll carry you on my back."

"Ah, Ah. Very funny," said Eva.

The bus driver turned off the air conditioning. While continuing its climb on a stone road to a parking lot a few miles higher, it skirted a succession of ruined walls. And finally appeared a glimpse of the remains of *Sans Souci* in the distance.

"These are the walls of the palace! These are the walls of the palace!" Caroline said to Eva and Ludovic.

"Yes!" replied Eva.

Caroline's heartbeat was quickening. She could no longer stay in place. In several positions she tried to take pictures.

"Calm down, Caro," said Ludovic. "We will go there later, remember?"

"Yes, but we won't be able to see it again from this angle."

The bus soon left everything behind. Banana trees, coffee shrubs, and other vegetation flourished on both sides of the road. Mr. Alexandre took the opportunity to remind the students of the reasons why fortresses like these were built throughout the country after the proclamation of independence.

"While we continue to climb the *Bonnet à L'évêque* mountain, I would like to take you exactly one hundred and ninety-four years back. Everyone on this bus, myself included are part of the 20,000 workers who took part in building the *Citadelle Laferrière*. Imagine not having any heavy machinery, tractors, trucks to transport the materials, nothing but only donkeys, horses, pickaxes, machetes, pikes, the strength of our arms, and a burning desire to survive!"

"Yaks!" whispered Caroline. "I am already dead."

"Me too," said Eva.

The bus arrived on a plateau. A few locals were waiting for them with their horses. A group of people with flutes, bamboos, and drums were playing a folk song. Ludovic pretended to be one of them by silently playing an imaginary cha-cha.

"We are digging day and night, but we are walking too; walk to where we are now. Our donkeys and our hoses, heavily burdened, carrying every stone, every beam, but also everything we need to eat and drink. "

The principal looked around. She had never seen so many paying so much attention on a school trip. The students were hanging on every word of Mr. Alexandre's lips.

The principal and the staff got out of the bus first to rent horses to carry the sandwiches and drinks they packed for lunch.

Eva was one of those who wanted to ride a horse. Caroline and Ludovic, on the other hand, started to walk very fast. They had decided to see who would get on top of the mountain quicker than the other.

"Children," advised Mr. Alexandre. "This is not about going fast here. Otherwise, you both won't make it at all. Take your time. We all have to build this fortress together."

Eva rolled her eyes and exhaled all at once.

"He's crazy!"

"I think this is very interesting!" said Ludovic who was helping her to climb onto the animal's back.

Mr. Alexandre took the lead. The music grew weaker and weaker with every step upward. The calm of nature was only interrupted by the sound of the hoofs trotting on the zigzagging stone path. Eva, the principal, and all those who had chosen to ride on horseback had to lean forward to reduce the pressure of gravity. Mr. Alexandre was barely out of breath.

"Look at Redingote," Caroline whispered to Ludovic. "He doesn't have a drop of sweat on his forehead."

"*Okap se kinan l, piwit an m* (Cap-Haitian is his own hood, child)," whispered back Ludovic in the regional accent of the area.

The sky was a deep blue for miles around. A cliff revealed a succession of green plateaus and hills. Mr. Alexandre stopped to allow everyone to take in the view.

"Wow!" exclaimed some students.

"What beauty!" said others.

Caroline suddenly was reminded of Eva's problems with heights. She turned to look at her cousin.

"Are you ok? Do you feel dizzy?"

"No. Not at all," Eva replied.

"Good," said Ludovic with relief.

The *Citadelle* was playing hide and seek with them. Each time the students thought they were reaching it, a turn in the road concealed it from view. Mr. Alexandre often stopped to admire the landscape and to help the group catch their breath.

Caroline was so busy photographing the horses, the other students and the nature all around her that she didn't notice that the road at a curve finally ended in front of the *Citadelle.*

"Here we are!" said Mr. Alexandre.

The fortress appeared in all its glory. The walls of the *Citadelle* rose before them, imposing, impressive, overwhelming. Pointed, the front of the fortress looked like a ship ready to leap into the void and sail on the clouds.

Caroline grabbed Ludovic's arm. A shiver seized her. Was it the fresh mountain air or the sheer emotion? Eva was still sitting on the horse, her mouth wide open, eyes on the impressive wall.

The principal, Eva and all those who were on horseback dismounted, looking dazed, under the spell of this gigantic building.

"We are at 2,900 feet above sea level. The Haitian engineer Henry Barre, under the supervision of General Henry Christophe, unfolds the blue prints. We watch them, standing there under the shade of those trees. We are 20,000 to arrive with rocks, bricks, and rudimentary tools."

"Sir, how many bags of cement are we going to use?" asked Ludovic completely immersed.

"None. Cement as we know it today did not exist. So, we are going to make our own mortar mix with quicklime, molasses, and the blood of local cows and goats."

Eva and a few other students gasped.

"This big wall is only held with that?" Caroline wondered.

"Not only that. To this mixture is added cows' hoof cooked with glue. That became a binder which will also give it strength. All this will become the mortar. Then, we will put stone over stone on over two acres for fourteen years. 2,000 of us will die in this cliff, but we are determined. We are determined to lay the foundations for this first country of the modern era established by free blacks."

Chapter 18

r. Alexandre climbed the last few feet leading inside the *Citadelle*. He walked quietly simulating the weight of the bricks they were figuratively carrying. Everyone's faces were drenched in sweat.

"Sir," asked Ludovic who was wiping his face, "why did you say General Christophe ordered this construction?"

"Remember: we are in 1805. Christophe is not yet king. He will proclaim himself Henry 1st in 1811. So, the construction started well before his reign."

"Was he already married to Marie-Louise Coidavid?" Caroline asked.

"Yes. And they had children."

"Jacques-Henry, François-Ferdinand, Francès-Améthyste, and Ann-Athénaïre," listed Eva.

Mr. Alexandre looked at Caroline and her cousin with a delightful smile.

"That's right."

The whole group was now facing large mahogany doors. Slowly and confidently, the teacher pushed them. The doors opened onto an extension of the stone path. The sloping path ran along the walls of the *Citadelle*.

"Impressive!" Caroline exclaimed.

On a terrace, a dozen cannons were lying singularly among pyramidal heaps of cannonballs.

"Mr. Alexandre, how did we get all these cannons and cannonballs up here?" asked a student.

"Do you remember how we got here?" he returned.

"On donkeys, on horseback, leaning on each other," replied another student.

"That's how! Now follow me, children! We are going to enter the fort!"

The teacher and the whole group walked through a second double door at a higher level. There were rooms on both sides of an open area. There were a succession of galleries and secret passages that gave the impression of a labyrinth. After a few contemplative steps, Mr. Alexandre stopped in front of what seemed to be an exist from a distance.

"Wow!" marveled the students.

Through an irregular geometric shape opening, a beam of light spread inside the room. Two sections of walls met transforming the space into a parallelepiped. Caroline looked up to the top of the one hundred-and-forty-feet tall wall. She felt like her neck was snaping in two. She grabbed her cousin's hand to show her some openings. They were in the form of windows distributed over five levels on the surface of the walls

"The *Citadelle* is made up of ten parts," echoed the voice of Mr. Alexandre. "We are currently in the *Batterie Coidavid.*"

"That's the queens maiden name," Caroline said.

"Yes. The various batteries mostly bear the titles of the royal family. This part is the one we saw when we arrived a little earlier. It's the one which looks like the bow of a boat. I believe this is one of the most beautiful parts inside the *Citadelle.* "

Mr. Alexandre and the group then took a wide stone staircase that led them to the inner courtyard. They felt like being crushed under the thickness of the walls. The ceiling, the floor, everything exuded an incredible strength.

Once outside, the teacher walked to the right towards a room. A grave painted in white stood silently in the middle of the sad room.

"What you are looking at is the tomb of Prince Noel, the brother of Queen Marie-Louise Coidavid."

"Why did they burry him here, sir?" asked a 12th grade student.

"Because it's here that he died accidentally during an explosion at the powder magazine."

Standing near a pile of canons in the outer courtyard, the principal opened her bag. Since she arrived in Cap-Haitian, she seemed to have a problem with her cell phone. There was no signal and the device was not receiving calls. Even from the summit of *Pic Laferrière*, the telephone remained silent. Displease, the principal put the device in her bag.

"Where did they find all these cannons?" she asked.

"These are, for the most part, the artillery that the French abandoned at the time of the war of independence," replied Mr. Alexandre. "The majority has been assembled here, to help defend the young nation. But the enemy will never come back. And all those cannons will forever remain silent."

Caroline looked at the walls of the impregnable fortress.

"So, what was the use for the *Citadelle* then," she asked.

"Very good question," said Mr. Alexandre. "Let's find out together."

The students followed the teacher. They did not want to missed any explanations from this 19th century trip. The teacher entered another room. While the large door of this one was linked to a corridor, on the right, there were at the bottom two openings in the wall.

"The *Cidatelle* was not just a fort. It was a whole complex that could easily house between 2,000 and 5,000 people at a time for an entire year. What you see there in this corner, is a baker's oven. The fort's pantry could store food for the entire regiment. The fort also had a kitchen, a foundry, a theater, places of recreation, a hospital, and so much more."

Mr. Alexandre left the room, walked along a corridor, and climbed two sets of brick stairs. Soon, the whole group found themselves on the seventh and final level of the *Citadelle*.

"Look here," said the teacher while pointing out a part of a roof made up of a succession of angles. "They could collect rain water which made the fort perfectly self-sufficient. It's quite a complex irrigation system. This water goes straight into basins and cisterns supplying the *Citadelle* with the vital substance."

"Fantastic! What an ingenious idea!" exclaimed the principal.

"Absolutely, ma'am. Just imagine to be able to envision such an architecture at the beginning of the 19th century, to make it stand without machinery in such time relates to the possibilities that were before them and beyond. Imagine this building designed by people who were believed to be brainless and only fit for slavery. To build this work in this way, the largest the American continent has seen back then is indeed extraordinary!"

The teacher gave the students a few minutes to ponder on this thought and admire the view. The road seemed small below. Caroline and the other students could not stop taking pictures. In turn, her cousin and Ludovic became photographers for a student, for two, for a group, for teachers, and finally for everyone. The background for those unforgettable moments had the panoramic sight of a succession of green mountains. In the distance, the blue of the sky tinted the mountains.

Mr. Alexandre, who was also taking pictures, put his camera away and led the group inside the fort. Quickly, he climbed a few steps and found himself on a terrace. Eyes wide open, Caroline, Ludovic and Eva were breathless by this spectacular view.

"In front of you," explained Mr. Alexandre, "you are contemplating the city of Cap-Haitian all the way to the bay. In this direction, you can see the *Limbé* and the *Soufrière de l'Acul* mountain ranges. In that direction, you have *Dondon*, *Fort-Liberté* and the sea. In all directions, there were no way to escape the watchful eyes of the *Citadelle*... You know, children, by including the *Citadelle* in the World Heritage, it's all this breathtaking nature which, too, becomes a landmark asset for humanity."

Nobody could take their eyes off the panoramic view; they could not stop filling their chests, their minds, their imagination with the air, the beauty, and the promises that the future might have brought to this small island. The teacher's voice brought them out of their reveries.

"Let's go children!" he said with authority.

Mr. Alexandre left the terrace, took another path, descended a few steps, and returned to the interior of the fortress. After a few detours, they were on the other side of the inner courtyard, just in front of an entrance whose façade was different from the others.

"The *Citadelle* was also built with the intention of being a palace of refuge for the king and his family in the event the city was attacked. This is what we are seeing now: The king's apartments which are called *Palais du Gouverneur* (The Governor's Palace)."

The architecture of the façade of the Governor's Palace was different from the other shapes of the fortress. At the end of a staircase with rounded steps, two cylindrical gatehouses reminded the presence of the soldiers who back then were permanently guarding the entrance to these apartments. The walls had no windows. They rose twice as high as the guards' houses mimicking the grandeur of the whole building.

Caroline grabbed her cousin's arm. Was it about this apartment that Thomas Madiou was referring to when he wrote about the looting of *Laferrière?* The teenagers thought that if they could only visit it, maybe they could see clues, find traces of something that could tell them where the treasure had been or where it could still be.

"Are we going to go in there?" Caroline asked as she approached the entrance.

"No. Access is prohibited to visitors," answered the teacher.

"There you go!" thought Caroline. If there were no secret, why stop people from visiting?"

Caroline looked at the teacher and said:

"Sir, it's here that Henry Christophe must have hidden the treasure."

Mr. Alexandre stared at the teenage girl.

"Definitely, Miss Lebrun, you are overflowing with imagination."

Caroline grew a little impatient. What she wanted was behind that door and she was denied access. She could not understand how a teacher who knew so much about the history of this fort, was totally ignorant of what they were looking for.

"Sir, it's not my imagination. The treasure did exist. It's just that we don't know where it is yet..."

All eyes were on Caroline. Aside from the trio, no one seemed to understand what she was referring to. An awkward silence seemed to even quieted the wind. Even Ludovic and Eva looked at Caroline, completely paralyzed by her last sentence.

"Ah, ah!" laughed Eva nervously. "It's true sir. My cousin has a big imagination."

Mr. Alexandre was not laughing. He looked at Caroline straight in the eye. He remembered telling her a few days earlier that it was a myth.

Mr. Alexandre had a kind of grin at the corners of his lips that almost looked like a challenge.

"And why are you so sure that this treasure existed?" he asked.

Caroline trembled a little. She had just realized that she had put herself in the spotlight.

"Well," said Caroline in a trembling voice, "when Henry Christophe died, they looted the *Citadelle* and the *Palais Sans-Souci...*"

"That's right..."

"A king always has things of value where he lives. Like jewelry, gold, paintings... For example, this fortress says it all."

"And what does it say?"

The students, the principal, and the other teachers were following the exchange as if they were watching a world cup soccer tournament. Ludovic and Eva were weighing each of the teacher's words, hoping to hear something that could help them in their research.

"The fact that they closed the access," said Caroline who had gained confidence in herself, "is the proof that they are trying to protect something. I believe that it was from this Palace that the generals carried off the treasure of the *Citadelle.* "

Mr. Alexandre smiled and was amused by Caroline stubbornness. He then addressed the whole group.

"What Miss Lebrun is referring to, is in fact a myth. For a long time, it was believed that within the walls of the Governor's Palace, Henry Christophe had buried a treasure of which only he and his right-hand man knew the location."

"And who was that right-hand man, sir?" Eva asked.

"The Earl of Citronade."

When they heard the name of the earl, everyone burst out laughing, except for Caroline, Eva, and Ludovic.

"But sir, wasn't that earl who looted the *Citadelle* alongside the generals?" asked Ludovic.

"Yes."

"And it's the same who married a lady-in-waiting at the *Palais Sans-Souci*, right?" asked Caroline.

"Absolutely. However, remember that it was the national treasury that was looted. No treasure was ever found. The *Citadelle* as you see it today was in ruins some time ago. We had to renovate it to be able to preserve it for future generations and to allow visits like the one we're having right now. So, if there was a treasure hidden in the walls or anywhere, we would have found it long ago, don't you think?"

Caroline looked at the teacher and felt sorry for him. How could he not know this part of the enigma? How could

Tonton Blain, a non-historian, alone held this secret? Caroline did not want to continue the discussion. She felt and saw in the eyes of Ludovic and Eva, like in her own, a renewed determination to find the truth.

The principal got closer to Caroline, touch her shoulder, and clapped.

"That was a great debate!" she said. "Hope you all learned a lot today about the *Citadelle.*"

The students also applauded enthusiastically. Ludovic looked at his watch. It was past noon. A light mist was beginning to fill the air.

"If you allow me ma'am," interrupted Mr. Alexandre, "we must go down. Because if the fog becomes too thick, we will have to sleep in the fort."

Chapter 19

The visitors were eating their lunches now inside the bus since they did not want to be stranded on the touristic site.

"You know what?" Caroline whispered to her cousin. "If *Laferrière* has no more treasures in it, I'm sure the walls of *Sans-Souci* will tell us something."

"That's what I was thinking too," said Eva between bites.

Going down the mountain was more tiresome than climbing it. Some students and teachers closed their eyes for a moment to rest. The music of the small group of folk singers, who were still there, filled the air. The driver was anticipating the time of departure and as soon as most of the students finished their meal, he started the bus and drove in the direction of the *Palais Sans-Souci.*

"Me," said finally Ludovic in a low voice, "I think we should find out who this earl really was."

The Earl of Citronade was indeed becoming a real enigma. If he was the right-hand man of Henry Christophe, he knew things that no one else knew. But what happened to him after the king died? Was he among those who looted the *Citadelle?*

"Here we are!" said Eva to her cousin while pointing to a large portal.

Caroline sat up to look. They were approaching the palace. Quickly, she finished her bottle of orange juice, wiped her lips with the back of her right hand and slung her camera around her neck. Once the bus parked in a parking area, Caroline left her seat and went out rapidly.

Mr. Alexandre took the lead. He adjusted his cap, cleared his throat, and walked towards the gate. Armed with precious information, he resumed his presentation.

"Henry Christophe proclaimed himself King Henry 1st in 1811. Quickly, he built several forts, fifteen palaces, and seventeen castles. But among all these constructions, the *Citadelle Laferrière* and the *Palais Sans-Souci* are by far the most beautiful achievements of this visionary King."

The teacher pushed the two carved iron doors that lead to the prestigious pathway. Caroline, Ludovic, and Eva raised their heads at the same time to admire the gates supported by four giant pilasters.

"This main entrance was reserved to the king, his family and the nobility," said the teacher while opening a folder. "I have brought you a copy of a picture painted during the time of Henry Christophe's reign by a young artist who was not older than you all. This copy will help you better understand our visit at the palace."

Caroline held out her hands to receive the sheet as if the answer she was looking for was in there. She first looked carefully at the copy before shifting her gaze to the ruins in front of her.

The ruins of the sumptuous residence were like an amphitheater throning in the middle of a surreal scenery. It was still standing on a slope in front of the verdant mountain ranges. It was standing in defiance of time and turbulent history.

"Henry Christophe had two goals in his life. First, he wanted to make sure that our country remains independent and free from threat of recolonization by the powers of that time. Second, he wanted Haiti to be at the level of all European and civilized countries."

Caroline walked in wonder towards the main entrance of the palace. The closer she got, the more she was in awe of this monumental palace. A few inches of grass surrounded rows of stones. As they walk, the path became a vast lawn in front of the castle.

"The *Palace Sans-Souci* was built between 1811 and 1813 on 6,800 acres. It was the most lavish palace that the Caribbean had ever seen. It is said that this palace was so extraordinary that it was nicknamed the Versailles of the Caribbean. As you can see, the building is not erected on flat ground. They had to level the hills and fill in the ravines to prepare the grounds."

Mr. Alexandre climb the semi-circular staircase of the palace's main stairs. Caroline adjusted her camera and took from below the pictures of the imposing building.

"The palace was built in a very eclectic style. That means a style made of a little bit of the many architectural movements that prevailed before the 19th century."

"Sir," said Eva, "why has the *Citadelle* remained as is but the palace is in ruins?"

"Because of two earthquakes. One happened in 1842 and the other in 1843. Although abandoned after the death of the king for twenty years, it was these two natural disasters that destroyed the palace completely."

With a gesture, the teacher told the group to follow him. Quickly Caroline climbed the fifteen steps, passed a few students who were in front of her, and stood next to the teacher.

"This was a large fountain," said Mr. Alexandre while pointing to a semi-circular alcove. "On each side on the pedestals that you see, there were sculptures of lions in bronze."

"Apparently, these lions were taken to Port-au-Prince and they are now in front of the courthouse," said the principal.

Caroline remembered seeing them more than once going to and from school. The lions were so impressive that they always give her chills.

"I don't think it's them, ma'am. Because the lions of the courthouse are not really in bronze."

"Really?" said the principal.

Mr. Alexandre took a few steps and pointed to the small houses stationed along the stairs.

"These towers that you see at the beginning of the stairs are guard houses. At this level, the stairs flip in two and a visitor could go either way until he arrived at the upper central level which is on top of this fountain."

Mr. Alexandre told the students to divide into two groups and climb the stairs of their choice. The students whispered among themselves. Some did not know which way to go. Others changed their minds, turn around, bumped into each other. Laughter and screams filled the air. Caroline and her group chose the staircase on the right. Together, Ludovic and Eva climbed the stairs fast, challenging each other to see who would arrive first.

Caroline, on the other hand, felt the need to stop and look at the brick steps. They were spacious enough for several people to walk on without fear of being cramped. Mr. Alexandre was now behind her. He was climbing the stairs with another teacher by his side. Caroline turned around suddenly and asked him:

"Sir, was it with the same mortar from the *Citadelle* that the palace was built?"

"Yes. The same mixture of quicklime and molasses."

Caroline then went towards the retaining walls. The decrepit walls were revealing the stones behind them. The teenage girl put her face closer to get a better look at what was biding the stones. Mr. Alexandre was amused by Caroline's curiosity. He calmly passed by her, smiling, avoiding to bother her.

When Caroline finally pulled herself away from the wall, she met the surprised face of the principal looking at her. She gave her a silly smile before hurrying up the few remaining steps.

Eva and Ludovic were already at the top level. They were facing the breathtaking view in front of them. Caroline took a picture of the sea looming in the distance between two mountains. Perfectly symmetrical, the facade of the building was a succession of arched openings. Three of them, surmounted by rounded beams, were actual doors that gave access to the entrance of the palace. The teacher clapped his hands to get everybody's attention.

"As you can see, the *Palais Sans-Souci* was built in a strategic location. Erected between mountains, it was hidden and perfectly self-sufficient. It was quite an organization. A town within the town of Milot. On this site, there was not only this castle, but also the royal library, a mint, a troop headquarters, printing shops, a stable, a hospital, an art school, a goldsmith, a farm, and so on. This is what the ruins you see around the palace were."

None of what the teacher was describing was important to Caroline. What she wanted was to enter the palace and see the queen's apartments. She was convinced that somehow, in the hollow of an alcove, she could discover a message, a clue left behind.

"The residence had three levels. During its construction, a system of pipelines was planned to carry water from the mountains to the palace by passing under the mezzanine. This system cooled down the interior of the house."

"Wow. It was like a natural air conditioning," Caroline wondered.

"Exactly. This water was channeled in such a way that the palace was equipped with all the modern comforts of the time."

Caroline felt transported back a century. She could see herself being invited and introduced to the queen. She could feel the silky ankle boots in her feet sliding delicately over the marble floors. She could imagine the mirrors, the mahogany furniture, the windows adorned with heavy curtains; she certainly could imagine the tall walls decorated with all the fine works of the *Royal Academy of Fine Arts*. She could see the light that was going through the stained-glass windows of this luxurious residence.

Mr. Alexandre walked throughout the adjoining rooms and finally headed towards the back of the palace. A ruined staircase came out of the ground floor to go to the first floor. Caroline climbed the stairs with her eyes. Eva and Ludovic came close to her and followed the path of the staircase also.

Mr. Alexandre stopped in front an arch door. The back of the palace opened onto vast green backyard. On either side, staircases were going down to scattered ruins. There were everywhere what appeared to be ponds.

"The queen was very fond of nature. Here, she built a botanical garden and a walking garden. They were both known as the *Jardin de la Reine* (the Queen's Garden). This beautiful fountain was part of it. Beyond the retaining wall, over there, there was also a swimming pool."

"*Wololoy* (Fancy)!" let out a student.

Caroline and the other students burst out laughing. Even in its ruined state, the *Palais Sans-Souci* was still magnificent.

"Sir, you never mentioned the queen's apartments. Where were they?" asked Caroline.

"Ah! That's exactly where we're going next."

The teacher returned inside the palace, crossed a few rooms, then turned to the left in the direction of the outside terrace.

"Of course, the Queen had her own suite in the castle. But beside that, there was also a place called the *Palais de la Reine* (The Queen's Palace). This building is now destroyed. Follow me kids!"

In a few steps, Mr. Alexandre brought the group in a big green space. This plaza framed by a sequence of rails was like a bridge between the *Palais Sans-Souci* and the

Queen's palace. In the middle, Caroline was attracted by a statue. It was the bust of an armless woman on a pedestal. A rope that ended with a laughing mask was slung over her shoulder. With high hairdo, broken nose and mouth, the white marble sculpture was leaning on the side, facing the back of the palace.

Mr. Alexandre stood by the statue and waited for students and teachers to form a semi-circle. Meanwhile, Eva, who had Caroline's camera, was taking photos of the bust.

"During the queen era, there were about fifteen statues all over the estate to adorn the gardens. These statues came directly from Italy. Unfortunately, this bust is the only one that was left. The others were looted."

The bust was near a star apple tree that was over a hundred years old. The students were amazed to see this old tree still standing. Not far away, a line of walls in ruins were facing it.

"This is all that remains of the Queen's Palace," said the teacher.

The facade with its arched openings was the only remnant of the queen's residence. Caroline, Eva, and Ludovic took their time to survey the area. By the visible lines on the ground, they could surmise the size of the rooms. The walls were a combination of stone and brick. The trio carefully looked around. But there was no clue. A little disappointed, they joined the group that was forming around Mr. Alexandre. He was talking about life in the 19th century. As she was listening, Caroline saw herself mingling with the guests during these evenings where music, literature and fashion were at the heart of conversations. She saw herself in a cotton muslin dress, her hair skillfully styled. She could hear herself laughing with the Queen, the princesses, the duchesses, the countesses, and other illustrious personages who must have traveled the world over to see this *Versailles of the Caribbean.*

The visit was ending. It was time to leave. Caroline turned around, looked up at the building, and gazed at the awe-inspiring ruins.

The teacher stopped a moment and said:

"Whether it is the *Citadelle Laferrière* or the *Palais Sans-Souci,* all was designed and built in the six years following the proclamation of independence. Children, do you understand what this means?"

A student standing next to Caroline raised her hand.

"Go ahead," encouraged Mr. Alexandre.

"I think it means that if people have the opportunity to do extraordinary things, they can achieve extraordinary things."

"Very good… Anything else?"

"Me," said Eva, "I think we were all born equal."

"Hmmm…. All born equal… This is indeed the testimony of our excursion. Every human on this earth has the right to dream and to make their dream come true. So, children never stop dreaming. But, above all, pursue your dreams. Do not let anyone put you down. You will go as far as you want to go, if and only if you believe in yourself."

Chapter 20

The visit to the *Palais Sans-Souci* was shorter than what Caroline and her cousin expected. They knew that the palace was in ruins, but they had never thought that bad weather and absence of a roof would have affected so much the survival of the monument.

Mr. Alexandre was standing in front of the bus and with a mechanical gesture, was encouraging the students to get back into the vehicle. Caroline and her group were almost at the end of the line. Soon, she noticed that the teacher's hands had stopped mobbing back and forth. Mr. Alexandre's face lit up. A childish smile appeared on his lips. Intrigued by this sudden transformation, Caroline turned her head in the direction of what was causing such an emotion in her teacher.

"Good God! Sir Brown?!"

This outburst from Mr. Alexandre rattled everyone. The students, the principal, and the staff stopped their progression to the bus to see who Mr. Alexandre was addressing.

An assured but slow eighty-year-old man was coming out of the tourists' and visitors' building located in front of the parking lot. Hearing his name, the old man shielded his eyes from the sun to better see the person uttering his name.

"George Alexandre?" he asked bewildered.

Mr. Alexandre walked toward the old man arms opened.

"Yes, Sir Brown! It's me!

"George Alexandre! Oh my!"

The old man hugged Mr. Alexandre before giving him a firm handshake.

"It's been so long!"

"Yes, it has", replied the teacher. "The last time I saw you, you were going to *Fort-Liberté* to visit your brother, am I right?"

"Exactly. What? Are you teaching here now?" asked the old man upon seeing the students.

"No. I still live in Port-au-Prince. We are on a field trip. Let me introduce you to our principal. Madam, this is Sir Brown, my mentor."

Sir Brown took off his straw hat and bowed slightly.

"Mr. Joseph Brown."

"Pleased to meet you."

"Sir Brown," continued Mr. Alexandre, "is a scholar in the history of our country. In fact, I would venture to say the whole Caribbean region. He *is* a living encyclopedia."

The old man put back his hat on his head, leaned on his cane, and smiled as he looked at Caroline and the last students who were boarding the bus.

"Oh!" said Mr. Alexandre, "These are some of our best seniors… children, say hello to Sir Brown."

"Good morning, Sir Brown," relied the students in unison.

Caroline looked at the old man. He reminded her of Tonton Blain. His gentle and elegant demeanor, his deep voice, and sparkling youthful eyes were just like his. His shirt was meticulously tucked inside his pants held up by a leather belt which color matched his shoes.

"Hello children."

"How sad that it's only now that we're meeting," said Mr. Alexandre. "We just finished our tour and are returning to the hotel."

"I hope you enjoyed your visit, children," said Sir Brown.

"Yes," admitted Eva.

"A lot," added Caroline.

"This beautiful trio here are true enthusiasts of Queen Marie-Louise," remarked Mr. Alexandre.

"Really! The Queen?" Sir Brown retorted. "It is not very common to find such interest."

"Absolutely. Miss Lebrun, Miss Baptiste, and Mr. Paul are so passionate about this subject that I'm starting to worry..."

"And why is that?" interrupted the old man. "I am sure that they are as curious as you were at their age. You forgot how many times your parents came, searching for you in my study. I too, back then, was worried about you. You refused to eat or to sleep. Your passion was solely history and... languages."

Mr. Alexandre made a face as he closed his eyes. Caroline and the other students could not stop laughing. They have never thought that their teacher was once a teenager like them. The principal also was smiling.

"You can feel the passion," she said. "He was the best guide for this trip."

"Thank you, ma'am."

The principal ordered the remaining students to board the bus. Caroline hastened to sit by the window. She wanted to see the old man one last time.

"Well…," said Mr. Alexandre sadly. "We have to go back to the hotel."

"Me too, I have to go back home… Where are you all staying?"

"The Auberge Laferrière."

"That's not too far from my home."

"Still driving the 1946 Nash Sedan?"

Sir Brown rolled his eyes.

"One of these days I will tell you the true story of this car… For now, it is kept in a garage. Nowadays, I walk and take public transportation. That keeps me in shape."

"So," wondered the principal, "you came here on public transportation?"

"Absolutely, madam."

"Then, please, ride with us. Since the hotel is not too far, we will drop you off at your house. This will make us all happy especially your friend here Mr. Alexandre."

Caroline pressed her face against the window. Her heart was beating faster. She was hoping the old man would accept the invitation. He was the person they needed. Only the seats in front of her were empty. This was where Sir Brown would have to sit. She would therefore find a way to talk to him and, at least, verify what he knew.

"Thank you. But I would like in return to invite you all for ice cream. It's very hot. There's a whole team of people at my house making homemade sorbet."

"Wow!" said Mr. Alexandre in astonishment. "Do you still have the ice cream shop on the boardwalk?"

"I am too old now. My children oversee the business. But everything is still done in the yard... I think your students will like that."

"Accept! Please accept!" Caroline was begging in her mind. Mr. Alexandre's face was radiant as if he was a teenage boy. Silently he turned to the principal, waiting for an answer.

"Your offer is very tempting, Sir Brown."

"Perfect!" said the old man.

"Let's go!" replied Mr. Alexandre cheerfully.

As soon as Sir Brown got inside the bus, Caroline realized that she will not be able to speak to him as she anticipated. Seated between Mr. Alexandre and the principal, the old man was going from one story to another. Caroline smiled as she listened to his deep voice. She had the impression of finding herself a few years back, around Tonton Blain on a Sunday, attentive to endless anecdotes he had accumulated during his many trips.

"Sir Brown," said the principal, "I'm a bit curious. Can I ask you a question?"

"Certainly, madam."

"Earlier, you introduced yourself as Mr. Joseph Brown. Why are you called *Sir Brown* then?"

The old man put a half-smile on his thin lips and turned to Mr. Alexandre. The teacher burst out laughing. A laugh so real, so spontaneous, that all the passengers on the bus leaned over to look in the direction it came from.

"Believe it or not," said Sir Brown, while pointing at the teacher, "it's because of this young man."

"Really!" wondered the amused principal.

"Yes. Georges has been always fascinated by languages and his father and I were good friends. So, one day, he must have been six or seven years-old, he came to my house and heard me talking about my great-great-grandfather who was American. He was an English teacher that everybody called Sir Brown. When I was telling that story, I was at that time an English teacher myself. So that is why he started to call me also *Sir Brown* and that is how the name stuck."

"What he forgot to say and that impressed me at that age was the fact that his grandfather was a teacher at the court of King Christophe," explained Mr. Alexandre.

Once she heard the name of the king, Caroline straightened up. Eva stopped chewing a candy.

"Did you hear that?" Caroline whispered.

"Sir Brown's great-great-grandfather worked for Henry Christophe!" repeated Eva.

Ludovic stopped talking to a classmate and looked at the girls. His eyes were saying it all.

"But, how did your great-grandfather end up here?" ask the principal.

"At that time Henry Christophe had made a name for himself outside of Haiti. Many colored people admired him. And the women all wanted to look like the queen. This is why when an invitation was launched for free black Americans to come and live in Haiti, Moise Brown, my great-great-grandfather, as well as his two sisters, decided to leave New Hampshire where they were already teachers and came to settle in Cap-Haitian to serve as English teachers in schools the king had just built."

The bus reentered the city. Mr. Alexandre was leading the driver to his friend's house. Caroline could not wait. She had a feeling that Sir Brown was a key to unlock some of the mysteries. She was eager to hear about his family and what he knew about Marie-Louise Coidavid. Caroline opened her bag to check that she did not forget Ludovic's copy of the drawing of the Espérances heraldry.

The bus slowed down quite a bit. Unlike the other streets, Sir Brown's neighborhood was rather deserted. His family owned several houses on the street. The bus stopped in front of a one-story house. It was an interesting house with four dovecotes and colored roof tiles. The ornate wooden doors and windows were wide opened. Mr. Alexandre helped Sir Brown to get out of the bus.

"Follow me, please," said the old man to everyone.

Mr. Alexandre made sure that no one stayed in the bus, the driver and his assistant included.

The living room's wood floor creaked under Sir Brown and his guests' footsteps. The old man led the group to a courtyard. Under an almond tree in the middle of the courtyard, several men and women were churning the last batch of ice cream. Young children were enjoying their generous portion in plastic cups. The children rushed to Sir Brown when they saw him. The grand-father hugged them and kissed their bushy hair.

One of Sir Brown daughters was the first to notice Mr. Alexandre.

"Georges!"

Mr. Alexandre walked up to her and kissed her energetically on the cheeks.

"Christine! What a surprise!"

"This is unexpected. What brings you here on this day?"

"I'm on a school trip."

A young man joined his sister.

"It must have been the ice cream," he said. "I'm sure of that."

"It's true your dad surely makes the best ice cream on that side of the country."

Mr. Alexandre turned to introduce the principal. But she was already seated on a rocking chair next to Sir Brown and was enjoying a soursop flavor. All the students were scattered all over the courtyard enjoying their vanilla, caramel, mango, papaya, passion fruit or coconut ice cream.

Sir Brown oldest daughter turned to the teacher and said in a low voice:

"Yesterday, he brought to the house a group of Canadian students."

"I think I know the group you're talking about. They are staying at the hotel."

"That's what keeping him young," replied Sir Brown's son.

After a few moments, Sir Brown noticed the absence of Caroline, Eva and Ludovic. They were not among the students who were under the almond tree. They were not with Mr Alexandre who was dwelling in souvenirs with his sons. Nor were they helping to dismantle the ice cream makers. After a few moments, the old man left his walking chair and decided to head for the living room.

The trio was indeed inside the house. They were staring at a portrait hanging above a piano. It was a large painting of a young woman wearing a high waist dress with puffed sleeves. A simple row of pearls adorned her neckline.

As they continued to explore the house, Caroline noticed the chandelier above. On the other hand, Ludovic was attracted by a large object on their right.

"It's my mirror," he whispered.

"Where?" Eva asked him while turning her head in all directions.

Ludovic pointed to a 19th century mercury coated mirror that was reflecting their profiles. The mirror was encased in a carved and gilded wooden frame. The top of the mirror was covered by garlands with ribbons that connected acanthus leaves and ended at the corners.

"Are you sure?" asked Caroline.

"Positive," replied Ludovic.

"How about the chandelier?" Caroline said. "It is identical to the ones we have at home."

Eva could not believe her eyes. Her cousin was right. It was the same entanglement of golden acanthus leaves and branches adorned with molded glass flowers. Caroline looked around the room. With its ten-foot-high ceiling, its wooden interior walls, the house was built in the 19th century.

Chapter 21

ir Brown was standing in the doorway between the gallery and the living room staring at them.

"You all are very fond of antiques," he finally said while approaching toward them.

The teenagers were startled by the voice behind them.

"Please! Don't be frightened," said Sir Brown reassuringly.

"Your house is very beautiful," said Eva.

"Thank you. Many of these things date back to Henry Christophe time. This mirror, for example, was in one of the rooms of the *Palais Sans-Souci*. And there were many more like that."

Ludovic's face turned pale. Caroline and Eva were equally stunned. The chandeliers in her bedroom and in her father office, Ludovic's mirror, the portrait of the queen and her daughters, are real antiques?

"Are they all from *Palais Sans-Souci?* The Sans-Souci in Milot?" Ludovic asked.

"Yes," answered Sir Brown. "My grandfather never recovered from the looting of the palace. He was at a turning point in his life."

"Why?" Caroline asked.

"He was secretly in love with one of the princesses. And all these events happened before he could officially declare his love."

Sir Brown drew their attention to the portrait above the piano.

"This is a picture of Princess Francès-Améthyste. She was also called *Madame Première*. This portrait was painted from memory by my grandfather after he realized that the Queen and her daughters were gone forever. It is one of the rare paintings representing one of the king's daughters. I wonder if it is not one of the only two in the world."

Caroline, Eva, and Ludovic got closer to the portrait. She was one of the three women in their painting. Eva smiled thinking that Sir Brown was so wrong in believing that this painting was the only one.

"Where did you see the other portrait, sir?" Ludovic asked.

"Not long ago in a catalog of an important art gallery in New York. This gallery had a portrait of the children of King Henry Christophe. In it you saw Jacques-Victor Henry along with Francès-Améthyste, and Anne-Athénaïre. Really, you should see this portrait. You would think, it's a photo taken on the spot!"

"And what is it doing there?" asked Caroline puzzled.

Sir Brown raised his hands in the air and let them fall with a sigh.

"You know children, a lot of things disappeared after the death of the king. Many of them got spread all around the world. And now, finding them more than a century later is a real problem."

"So, your great-great-grandfather never saw *Madame Première* again?" asked Eva.

"Yes, he did."

Sir Brown proceeded in telling them how Moses Brown traveled to England to see the Queen and her daughters once more. How he found them isolate, weakened but dignified.

"They lived at the time in Weymouth Street in London. Their presence in the city was known. But they kept to themselves. My grandfather seized the opportunity to declare his flame. But the princess taught he was mocking her or trying to take advantage of her situation. Finally, he returned to Cap-Haitian and married the daughter of one of the dukes a few years later. The princesses, on the other hand, never married."

"And what about the queen? She never remarried?" asked Caroline.

"No. And she was never able to return to the country either. She died alone in Italy."

"Italy? I thought they went to England after the king death," Eva said.

"Yes, that's true. However, Italy had a warmer climate. This is why after some time in London, they settled in Pisa. But the youngest of the princesses was already seriously ill and eventually died. Shortly after, *Madame Première* would die from a stupid fall."

> *Imagine our suffering for not being near you and able to elevate our cause...*

These sentence from the acrostic came back to Caroline. She felt a deep sadness. She could see the Queen leaving her native country in anguish; traveling for weeks over the Atlantic Ocean and finding herself in England. She could feel the cold, the rain, the dampness crippling her in her very soul. She could experience her coping, surviving in a foreign culture, and finally taking refuge in Italy and dying there alone, in exile, without ever seeing her native land again… What a miserable final journey!

"So, the whole king's family disappeared just like that?" Ludovic asked.

"Just like that…"

Caroline was tensing up. She had a burning question on her lips. Having heard the answer more than once, she felt a certain anguish just thinking about it. But she had to ask it.

"Sir, is the *Citadelle*'s treasure real?"

"Well…" said Sir Brown in a deep breath. "They always said it is a myth. That was what I thought myself for years. But, the more I think about it these last days, the more I wondered…"

"It could be somewhere?" asked Caroline

"Well," said the old man while turning to Ludovic. "As you must have discovered, women like beautiful things, right?"

"Yes, Sir Brown," answered the teenage boy with a smile.

"So, imagine the adornment of these ladies when they held parties at the Palace or when they were having dignitaries over. Of course, they didn't just have a few jewels and the king just a few silver coins. I am certain that they had a treasure trove of jewelry, gold, precious stones somewhere, hidden from prying eyes... And then think about the crowns..."

Eva and Ludovic shook their heads in approval. With pursed lips, they could barely contain the happiness that was rising within them. Caroline let out a little cry of joy while clinging to her cousin. It was the first time that an adult supported their logical claims.

"Then, do you think they are somewhere?" asked the teenage girl.

"Maybe... I'll have to explore the subject a little more. It's too bad that you all don't live here. I feel that you would have certainly helped me..."

"Oh, yes!" Eva said.

"Sir Brown, who was the earl of Citronade?" asked Ludovic. "Mr. Alexandre told us that he was the king's right-hand man."

The old man heaved a sigh and suddenly became serious.

"We need to stop saying that. This man betrayed the king. I myself long ago stopped calling him Earl. People like that you simply call them by their name. And that's all!"

"And what was his name?" asked Caroline anxiously.

"Louis-Achille Simon," replied Sir Brown.

The old man while talking was taking his glasses which he had left over an armchair, he did not see Caroline's mouth parted with emotion. Was the earl the Simon that Ludovic's family tree was referring to? How could that be since that one was born in 1826? Could he be a relative?

"Did the earl have children?" Ludovic asked urgently.

"Yes. It seems that he had many. Apparently, one was even called François-Ferdinand after the king's son," said Sir Brown.

Caroline thought she was going to have a heart attack. Thus, the François-Ferdinand Simon in Ludovic's list was the son of the Earl of Citronade, the same one who was the king's right-hand man.

Ludovic could no longer contain himself. His grandfather was from Cape-Haitian. According to his list, he was part of this genealogy. Maybe Sir Brown knew him.

"Sir, did you know Xavier Paul? When he was young, he used to live just outside of the city."

Sir Brown leaned on his cane with both hands trying to remember.

"Xavier Paul..." he repeated pensively. "I think so. A man who had your complexion and who was almost as tall as you."

Ludovic nodded yes.

"He was my grandfather."

"Really? Now I understand where your curiosity comes from."

"How so, Mr. Brown?" Ludovic asked.

"Well as far as I remember, Paul was just as enamored with Cape-Haitian history as I have been. We formed a club just to research the royal treasure. We spent countless hours speculating, comparing what we discovered..."

"What did you find?" Eva asked.

"Back then? Not much. We were young and a bit crazy. Your grandfather left for Port-au-Prince and the others have moved on. How is he? Has he become a collector like me?"

Caroline looked furtively at Ludovic. A hint of sadness could be seen in his eyes.

"He died recently," replied the young man.

"Ah!... I am sorry to hear that."

"Thanks. He collected a few coins and he had a mirror like the one in your living room," said Ludovic with a beating heart.

Sir Brown's eyes widened. His face lit up as if transported back to distant memories.

"Really? He kept his? His brother and I had found these mirrors at the home of an old lady who didn't quite understand their value and who wanted to get rid of them… You know, we were so immersed in the story of Henry Christophe. We decided that when we have children, we would give them the first names of the king's children."

Sir Brown shook his head from side to side while bursting out laughing. He walked to adjacent room and signaled the children to join him. He was walking with determination. He could not see the extent of the amazement that had gripped the trio. He could not see Ludovic panting with emotion and Caroline, and Eva holding him. They were so happy to see the family tree making sense again.

"You said his brother was there when you bought the mirror?" Ludovic asked a bit out of breath.

"Yes, his half-brother, François-Ferdinand."

"François-Ferdinand Blain?" said Caroline surprise.

"Yes… It was he who was the first to say that the names of the king's children had to be perpetuated. He himself had the first name of the eldest son of Henry Christophe who died before he became a monarch."

Sir Brown paused for a moment and looked at Caroline straight in the eye.

"Did you know him too?" he asked puzzled.

"Yes. He worked in my family Law firm until his death."

"Ah!... So, he too became a lawyer. Blain left Cape-Haitian a few years after his father married Paul's mother. That was his second marriage. And we never saw him again."

Sir Brown sat down in an armchair behind the desk. He seemed for a moment immersed in memories that were both happy and painful.

This avalanche of information was more than they bargain for. Caroline understood better why Tonton Blain persisted in wanting to name her father and her. Having had no children, it was a bit by adoption that he wanted to honor the pact of this youth club.

The old man took a deep breath.

"What a small world," he said finally. "Well, children! Let me show you something."

The room was the host's study. A large map was hanging on the wall. It was a reproduction of Cape-Haitian in colonial era. There were books everywhere, over desks, on shelves, over chairs. The oldest ones were catalogued and put out of reach in glass bookcase. Caroline found the smell of the old papers and books exhilarating.

Sir Brown opened one of his desk drawers and took out a scrapbook. In it were copies of old newspapers.

"This looting of the *Citadelle* and the *Palais* Sans-*Souci* made it hard to find even a tiny part of what was lost. To understand just a little the splendor of King's Henry reign, I am going to read parts of a newspaper published in England on December 13, 1811. The newspaper speaks of a seizure made by the British customs. The seizure involved of a shipment intended for the court of Christophe. This is what was written on the order: *The seizure made at the Custom house some time ago, of the valuable articles intended for the Emperor of Hayti, has excited much curiosity... A crown set with diamonds rubies and emeralds. A case containing a gold cup. One pair of gold spurs. One row of gold beads and tassels. One diamond collar. One box containing sundry diamond and gold pins, brooches, earrings, and watches. Seven diamond tiaras. Diamond lockets, pins and rings. One Chrystal with tassel...* etc."

"Wow!" Eva exclaimed.

"But Sir Brown, why did they seize all that?" asked Caroline.

"Under the pretext that the total value has not been properly assessed. But the shipment was released and finally arrived in Haiti."

"Were you able to find some?" Ludovic asked.

"Just a very few. Over the years, we were able to recover certain things that were circulating in the city and elsewhere. We were able to find the entire collection of the *Gazette Royale* and the *Almanack Royal d'Haiti*."

"What is that?" Caroline asked.

Sir Brown opened another drawer of his desk and searched for a moment before finding a booklet. He handed it to Caroline.

"They were publications that kept people up to date back then with the latest news of the kingdom. What I gave you is such a publication. It's not an original, but a copy."

Caroline, Eva, and Ludovic got closer to see.

"*Almanach Royal D'Hayiti pour l'année 1814. Au Cap-Henry, chez P. Roux, imprimeur de Sa Majesté.* "read Caroline.

"The Almanac is from the year 1814 and printed by his majesty's publisher P. Roux," said Eva.

Caroline turned the pages and was amazed how well the kingdom was organized. *La Maison de la Reine* and *l'Éducation des Princesses Royales* (The House of the Queen and the Education of the Princesses) had a section devoted to them and latest endeavors.

"These are the coast of arms of the King," recognized Ludovic on the cover page.

Sir Brown looked at the young man with an amazed gaze.

"Well, well! You know a few things! Did your grandfather tell you about it?"

Ludovic took a moment before answering. He wished his grandfather told him something, anything.

"No," he replied in a sorry tone of voice. "Mr. Alexandre showed us once what the coat of arms looked like"

"I see. But you know that these were not the only ones in the Kingdom of Christophe, right?"

"We know. Mr. Alexandre also told us about the heraldry of some noble families."

Sir Brown took out of his pocket a handkerchief and revealed a key hidden within it. He opened the glass bookcase and pulled out a book.

"You know, Henry Christophe had a big court. There were three princes, nine dukes, nineteen earls, thirty-six barons and eleven knights. All had their own heraldry…

Flip through this book and you'll see what I'm talking about."

"Oh!" said Caroline after a moment. "The queen also had her coat of arms?"

"Yes," replied Sir Brown. "Hers was very close to that of the king. But as you see, there were modifications that made it more feminine. Like, the two floral scrolls that surround the royal crown."

Footsteps drew Sir Brown's attention to the open door. Mr. Alexandre inquisitive eyes appeared in the doorway.

"There you all are," he said.

"Your students are a delight!" Sir Brown replied with an admiring look. "I think I will keep them with me, especially Ludovic and Caroline. His grandfather and a friend of Caroline's family were both my childhood friends."

"Really?" said Mr. Alexandre in astonishment. "You both never told me that. So that's why you are so curious."

Caroline and Ludovic felt a little embarrassed not revealing the reasons for their questions the last few months.

Mr. Alexandre looked at his watch.

"We must leave Sir Brown. The children need to be ready for a show tonight."

Sir Brown opened a drawer and pulled out another booklet.

"Before they leave, I have one last thing that I would like to show them."

The old man had suddenly a very serious look on his face. He walked as quickly as he could to a cabinet, opened it with another key, and pulled a carboard box.

"A few years ago, I was in Europe at an auction. I was able to obtain this."

Delicately, Sir Brown took out a fan which he opened before passing it to Caroline. Filled with emotion, the teenage girl first admired the ivory frame that supported the lace golden sheet. In the middle, a silk cloth featured a gallant scene that was held in a garden.

"The fountain you see in the painting is that of the Queen's Garden, which you have probably visited at the *Palais Sans-Souci.* "

"Wow," Eva said.

Caroline passed the fan to her cousin.

"Well, Sir Brown," said Mr. Alexandre, "I am jealous. You never showed me this."

"That's what happens when you abandon a friend," reproached the old man.

Sir Brown's daughter came into the study, obviously intending to end what seemed to be a secret meeting.

"Dad!" she said reproachfully. "You have to let them go."

Sir Brown turned to the trio and gave them a wink.

"Children, keep the copy of the *Almanac* and the *Gazette Royale* of October 1815. That will be your little souvenir from Cape-Haitian."

Chapter 22

The hotel was indeed very close to Sir Brown's house. In less than ten minutes the bus was in the parking lot, dumping its passengers.

The buffet was barely set up in the restaurant. The students had to eat quickly before going to their rooms. Caroline, Eva and Ludovic sat together around a small table. They wanted to scream their joy.

"Can you imagine?! A club where they only collected things from the kingdom of Christophe!" Caroline said.

"It must have been very easy," replied Ludovic. "My grandfather's time was closer to the events that had taken place here."

"Too bad Tonton Blain couldn't keep his mirror."

"But at least we now know what all these objects sculpted with so much art that the novel was talking about are", reminded Ludovic who was finishing his meal. "The paintings, the chandeliers, the beautiful fan, the books..."

"We also know," said Eva, "why the queen said that she could not leave her daughters in the cold and melancholy. Anyway, I did not climb *Puilboreau* mountain for nothing."

"You'll have to be brave again. Because we have to go back home," reminded Caroline.

"God have mercy! Did Aunt Micheline put some sleeping pills in the first aid kit?"

The fear Eva felt the day before came back on her face. Caroline and Ludovic burst out laughing.

Ludovic looked at his watch. There was not much time left to get ready for the promised "unforgettable evening."

Once in their room, Caroline and her cousin felt the weight of the excitements of the day. Eva threw herself on the bed while Caroline dragged herself to the bathroom. While in the shower, she thought back to a few months earlier. From the beginning when Ludovic dropped his piece of paper in the library, the research that ensued the mystery, the rollercoaster of emotions they have felt were the most exciting moments she ever lived.

Caroline got out of the shower and went into the bedroom to wake up her cousin. Eva painfully got out of bed and went to the bathroom.

Pensively, Caroline was getting ready. Something was bothering her still. The message in her novel was typed but the one from the painting and the sentence which began Ludovic's list were written by the queen herself in her own handwriting. How would Tonton Blain and Mr. Paul both know the queen? How could the queen have given them two separate messages? There is also the obvious fact that the queen died in 1853, long before the two brothers were born.

Caroline pulled out the chair in front of the desk and sat down. She reached for her cousin's makeup bag in search of a nail clipper to cut a cuticle around her index finger that was hurting her.

"Good God, Caroline!" cried Eva coming out of the bathroom.

"What's the matter?" her cousin replied.

"No way you go out looking like that!"

Caroline was wearing a long black skirt and a gray blouse. The sleeves were rolled up. She pulled her hair back into her usual bun with a red elastic ribbon. Her sneakers were barely concealed and her camera around her neck looked like a big chain.

Without giving her cousin time to place one more word, Eva undid Caroline's hair, separated it in two, and began to braid it artistically. From her bag filled with hair accessories, she took a few pins adorned with shiny stones, and arranged them as in a princely wat around her head. Caroline took out of the luggage a hand mirror and look at herself. She liked the braid crown and the few strands of hair that her cousin let hanging on her temples and her neck.

Suddenly, Caroline turned around.

"No way! I don't deal with makeup!"

"Well, there's always a first time. Come on Caro! Let me prep you! The program said "Unforgettable Evening". So, we must be unforgettable too, don't you think?"

Caroline gave in. Eva barrowed her golden ballerina flat. When Caroline looked at herself in the bathroom mirror, she was amazed at the transformation. Her rosy cheeks, the copper tone on her eyelids, the glossy shine of the lip gloss made more than what she ever put on.

Eva got ready in no time. She prepared in advance her wardrobe. She too had braids that dangled on the side with pearls. The theme of her ensemble was a navy-blue shade that donned her skirt and asymmetrical top. She accessorized her outfit with a silver bracelet on her forearm. Her shade of makeup was an almost violent red.

Ludovic was already seated on the bus, joking with some other students. The two girls entered the bus and brought with them a sweet fragrance of youth. They were the only ones who wore colorful dresses. Everyone else were in a boring white shirt or blouse and black pants or skirt. Ludovic watched the girls finding a sit. His eyes shined brightly at Caroline sight. It was the first time he saw her wearing makeup.

Mr. Alexandre stood stiff in a black suit and a white shirt without a tie. He was standing next to the principal who was wearing a floral maxi dress. The principal addressed the eager students.

"Children, our Unforgettable Evening will be simply that - UNFORGETTABLE! We are going to attend a show that local high school students from Cap-Haitian and Milot have put on. This show will be presented at the *Palais Sans-Souci!*"

Caroline and Eva exchanged a cheerful look. They were going to see this extraordinary Palace one last time.

"There will be a lot of people there," continued the principal. "Each teacher will lead and be responsible for a group. You must stay with the members of your group."

The principal red from a list the different groups. Luckily, the trio was in Mr. Alexandre's group. Ludovic barely heard the instructions. He could not take his eyes off Caroline. It seemed that time stopped for him.

When the bus finally arrived in front of the *Palais Sans-Souci* Caroline got off quickly. She felt as if she had been freed from a cage. She breathed deeply. She was going to disappear in the crowd. But Ludovic followed her off the bus also quickly.

"You are so beautiful!" he finally let out.

Was he crazy? Beautiful under this ton of make-up? Caroline felt a fire burning on her cheeks.

Ludovic stare was embarrassing her. The teenage girl lowered her eyes. She taught she looked like a *madigra* (a clown). She taught she should have never let Eva put that plaster on her face. The blouse and the skirt she had chosen at first were more than enough. And then these shiny shoes were so ridiculous! Caroline wished she could disappear.

"Thank you," she said none-the-less.

Eva smiled. She was proud of her work. She was able to transform her cousin into one of the princesses of Marie-Louise Coidavid Christophe court, at least for a night.

"You're very pretty too, Eva," said Ludovic who suddenly realized Eva's presence.

"Yeah, yeah. Thanks," Eva replied rolling her eyes.

A small crowd of people was heading towards the entrance of the palace. The vast lawn in the front was transformed into an open-air theater with dozens of rows of chairs encircling the stage.

Perched on top of its mountain in the background, the illuminated *Citadelle Laferrière* offered a dazzling spectacle to the surrounding valley. Caroline tilted her head and saw the thousands of twinkling stars in the darkness of the sky. Neither she, nor her cousin, nor Ludovic could speak. They let themselves be guided, seated, and amazed. They read the program Mr. Alexandre gave them.

"The queen's coat of arms," recognized Caroline on the cover of the pamphlet.

"It's a play," indicated Ludovic.

"Oh, wow!" wondered Eva.

Suddenly behind them, a rhythmic sound of drums rose in the still night. On both sides of the lawn, characters dressed as 19th-century footmen lit lines of firecrackers. The exploding lights spread to the fan-shape staircase. While the front of the palace remained in darkness, the interior was suddenly illuminated, giving glimpses of garlands decorating the arched openings.

Then the music stopped. Complete silence filled the air. A few rapid sounds followed by three separate distinct ones came out of the palace. Then, the lights got out. The façade of the palace was illuminated now by projectors. A young man, dressed in the English fashion of the 1800s, appeared at the entrance of the palace. His voice carried far by a microphone.

"Parents, guests, ladies, and gentlemen. The play you are about to see was conceived by our seniors. Students from 9th to 11th grades from three different schools will join them in performing the play. It is conceived in the style of the play *Les Femmes Savantes*, written by the famous Molière, a French playwright. It is in three acts. It will depict life at the *Palais Sans-Souci* and the events that followed the death of the king."

A baroque musical piece, typical of the 19th century, began to play as soon as the narrator exited. Caroline looked around to see where the music was coming from. Light from a projector focused her attention to the esplanade that connected the castle to the Queen's Palace. But quickly, sounds of hooves and wheels came from the gate. An open carriage, trimmed in gold, steered by two brown horses, made its entrance. Garlands linked their mounts to the carriage.

"It must be the royal family," Caroline whispered.

"The one with the biggest crown must be the queen," added Eva.

The lights, the colors, the costumes, the music amazed Caroline and her cousin. As the scenes progressed, the character of Queen Marie-Louise became more and more prominent. Caroline shivered at one of the final scenes describing a last ball at *Sans-Souci*.

When the queen opened the ball with the *Prince Royal*, violins, flutes, and drums were playing a *contredanse*, a French colonial dance. From quick, elegant, and light steps, the *contredanse* turned into madness, entwining the feet of the royal family. Screams rose from everywhere. Hands that simulated the swelling ground up gripped the dancers, pulling them into the bowels of the earth. When the lights turned back on again, the queen was standing alone in silence, in a dark blue dress with dark gloves. She spoke in a deep, trembling voice.

"Call me Majesty no more. My misfortunes have detached me from all the vanities of this life. From now on, call me simply Madame Christophe."

Caroline's lips quivered. Tears were streaming down her cheeks. Eva let off a scream. She too was crying.

Chapter 23

n the following Sunday, at dawn, the bus left Cap-Haitian for Port-au-Prince. The return home was less exciting. The occupants of the bus slept through it all. It was late afternoon when they pulled into the courtyard of Audubon School.

Parents were already waiting for their children for more than an hour. Caroline, Eva, and Ludovic got off the bus thanked the principal, Mr. Alexandre, and the other teachers for the memorable trip. They retrieved their luggage, crossed the street, threw their belongings in the trunk of Caroline's parents' car before letting themselves fall in the back seat.

"So," how was the trip?" inquired Caroline's father.

"Great!" Eva said.

"The best!" Caroline added.

"Extraordinary!" Ludovic blurted out.

Amused by this unexpected choir, Dr. Lebrun looked at her husband and burst out laughing.

"Well kids!" she said, "tell us some more."

Caroline wasted no time to start talking. Though tired, she has been waiting impatiently for the moment to tell her parents about the wonders they had seen. And then there was also this intrigue that made them dream and kept them much excited during the whole school year.

The trio was in full story mode when a little music caught their attention. Caroline unsuccessfully searched for the source of the sound. The radio was not on. They were going too fast to catch a persistent sound from the street. Her mother looked in her bag.

"It's not mine," Dr. Lebrun said. "It must be yours."

"No," Mr. Lebrun replied. "It sounds like the music you chose for your phone."

"Wait! Am I hearing correctly? You bought a cell?!" Caroline exclaimed.

"Yes and yes," replied her father in a low voice.

Dr. Lebrun took a cell phone out of her bag and began a conversation with someone. While continuing her rather dull conversation, she pulled out of her bag her husband's phone which was identical and passed it to her daughter.

Caroline, Eva, and Ludovic have wondered if they would ever have one in their hands someday. The device opened like an envelope. A small antenna sticking out of it.

"Please," said Mr. Lebrun. "Do not call anyone. Minutes are expensive."

The trio just shook their heads in agreement.

"Wow!" wondered Eva.

"They say there are even models where you can see the people you are talking to," said Ludovic.

"You're kidding!" replied Eva.

"I am serious."

Caroline lifted her head up and slid forward to move closer to her parents.

"You bought one for me too?" she asked.

"Noooo," said her father with a little smile. "You may get yours if you pass the national exams. And that's maybe."

"Maybe?" wondered Caroline. "We will definitely pass!"

"Ok. I like that... So, this trip..."

The story of the excursion to Cap-Haitian continued until very late in the evening that day. However, to the dismay of her parents, the recounting lasted for weeks end. The obsession with this trip went so far as to make it almost impossible for Caroline, her cousin, and Ludovic to revise for their *Bac* exams. Each work session began and ended with memories of Cap-Haitian. Naturally, the auspicious date arrived. The trip to the Northern Kingdom helped Eva produce a history essay of a quality she would have thought impossible. The trio obtained good grades in all subjects without any difficulties. The summer vacations were then very welcomed.

The first weekend of summer, Caroline, her cousin and her mother were seated on the porch, when her father came home with two small shopping bags. He handed one to each girl. Intrigued, Caroline and Eva looked inside and saw each a gift box. Frantically, they tore the wrapping paper.

"Ah!" they shouted at the same time.

Caroline embraced her father while Eva covered her aunt with kisses. Caroline not only received all the materials required to start her first art class the following Saturday but also another gift. At the bottom of her bag, there was a small and compact box. Caroline carefully opened it. A dark gray device was in side. It was her cell phone. It was so light and small that she could easily put it in her pocket. It was the same model that the principal owned. She turned it on. The connectivity was already established.

After admiring her cousin's gift, Eva also carefully opened her box. She could not believe what she saw: a pair of silver dangling earrings. She rushed to a mirror to admire them in her ears. As she walked back onto the porch, the movement of the pendant and its diamond-cut finish casted bright streaks of light across her face.

"You look very beautiful" complimented her aunt.

"Thank you, Tati! I really like it!

Caroline meanwhile, was browsing through the ringtones. After listening to over a dozen, she made her choice. Then she filled the contacts with Ludovic's number, her parents' cell phones, and some other friends. Eva and her tried the different games installed on the device.

"We should have had this phone when we were in Cap-Haitian!" Caroline exclaimed.

"But the network doesn't yet cover the whole country," informed her father.

"Ah, so that's why the principal couldn't use hers!"

Caroline recounted how the principal was upset at the *Citadelle Laferrière* when she noticed that even so high up, her phone remained dead. The two cousins then began for the umpteenth time the story of their school trip.

Like every day, since their return, their stories were always about a part that they taught they forgot to mention; but, as always, their excitement never brought anything new. Nevertheless, Dr. Lebrun never got tired of hearing the same thing especially when Caroline was adding mimes to the stories. Her mother could not stop laughing

"Dad!" exclaimed Caroline. "Do you know that Sir Brown was Tonton Blain friend?"

"Yes... you already told me."

"He's the one who gave us a copy of the king's almanac," Eva added.

"You know, Tonton Blain had a copy of this book. Several originals, if I'm not mistaken."

"Really?" wondered Caroline.

"Do you know what he did with them?" asked Dr. Lebrun.

"No. There are a bunch of things that I used to see all the time in his house. They disappeared after his death and some even before," said her husband.

"Like what, dad?"

"You told me about a mirror you saw at Sir Brown's house. Well, he too had one..."

"Maybe he gave it to someone," said Eva.

Caroline sat up straight on her walking chair. The same question she had asked a hundred times and only Sir Brown seemed to understand came to her mind. She now wanted to ask it to her father. It would be great if Tonton Blain spoke to him about it, if Tonton Blain also believed in the same cause. But a persistent knock at the entrance gate prevented Caroline from asking.

"Where are they?" her father asked, looking around with his eyes for his employees.

"Let's go see," said Eva pulling Caroline by the arm.

The two girls ran to the front gate. Ludovic was there. He was about to leave when the two cousins opened the door for him. He blushed a little when he saw Caroline head pop up first. Since that unforgettable evening, Ludovic seemed to have never forgotten the way Caroline looked that night. Though she felt that her makeup turned her into a *mardigra* queen, she was, unbeknownst herself, a lost princess. At moment, she read in his eyes some kind of discovery that she would have liked him to forget.

"Come on in!" said Caroline.

"No. I can't stay long. I have to go on an errand for my mom. I know Eva is leaving for Canada in a few days. I stopped by to give you a little present. Don't forget us so soon and our famous treasure hunting!"

Caroline and Eva opened the folder. In it, there was a copy of the Espérance heraldry.

"Thank you. So, just like that, I'll be leaving without ever seen your mirror?" Eva asked.

"If her majesty wants to come over, it would be easier" said Ludovic in a bow. "You saw its size when we were at Sir Brown's house, right?"

"Yeah. The size of your head," teased Caroline.

The trio burst out laughing. And like every time they have met, they talked about their trip to Cap-Haitian. Ludovic suggested that, in a few years, they should go back there to spend some time exploring the city with Sir Brown.

Once Ludovic left, Caroline and Eva returned to the porch. As they passed a blooming rosebush, the two girls delicately cut a rose for their room.

The parents had already both disappeared. Caroline and her cousin settled on the rocking chairs. Caroline rocked back and forth while fanning herself with a magazine. The typical sweltering temperature of the summer months was in full swing. The sun was a burning furnace. Nothing could cool the air. It was during this season that Caroline understood best why the houses had such high ceilings back then with double pan doors and windows and jalousies like those of the houses she saw in Cap-Haitian.

"Are you and Natalie friends again?" Eva asked.

Caroline took a deep breath before answering.

"No... She was supposed to leave for New York yesterday and she didn't even call me... I think she really loves him..."

"But, thank God, he doesn't... Anyway... I think Ludovic and you get along preeeetty well..."

"Yeah, yeah..." replied Caroline with an embarrassed smile. "Natalie would eat me alive!"

"Ludovic doesn't care about her!"

"Who doesn't Ludovic care about?" asked Caroline's mother.

Dr. Lebrun was back on the porch with a glass of papaya juice in hand. She had only heard part of the conversation.

"No one special," answered Eva quickly.

While positioning herself on a rocking chair, Caroline's mother saw the copy of the drawing her daughter had on her lap.

"That's a good drawing. What is that?"

"The heraldry of a family from Cap-Haitian," her daughter replied spontaneously.

Dr. Lebrun took the paper and looked at it closely. It was just then her husband reappeared on the porch. He was in his jeans, swinging his car keys from one hand to the other.

"Does anyone need anything?" he asked.

"Look at that, honey… Doesn't this look familiar to you?"

Mr. Lebrun came closer to his wife.

"Mmmm…It looks like the drawing which was in Caro's room."

"Exactly!"

Caroline almost fell over the rocking chair.

"And where was it?" she asked anxiously.

"In the original molding of your windows."

Caroline looked at her cousin with dazed eyes. Didn't they discover it all? She was confused. She did not understand what was happening.

"It's the heraldry of a family that was related to Mr. Paul!" she informed.

"Really?" her father wondered.

Mr. Lebrun pursed his lips before shrugging his shoulders.

"After all," he said, "Tonton Blain and him were half-brothers, right? Of course, they had relatives in common. Now, does anybody need anything?"

Caroline and Eva shook their heads no.

"Just a jar of *Manba* (peanut butter) for the children," answered his wife. "Oh! There is something else I need…. Let me go with you."

"Alright. But I must stop by the auto shop first."

Caroline and Eva rushed upstairs to the second floor. Standing in the middle of the room, they imagined the Espérance heraldry above the frames of the two large windows. They could not believe all this time the heraldry was once in their bedroom. Could this mean that their search is not over?

Caroline thought about the message behind the painting that Tonton Blain gave her.

Lest we stop searching, the distance between us
Or the sadness in our hearts will be the only
Unique way to deny our cause its denouement…

Tonton Blain was buried a hundred feet underground. Was it this distance that separated them? She wanted to continue searching. But what exactly?

"Ah!" said Eva. "*All these objects fashioned with such artful hands…*"

"But," said Caroline, "we found them all. Remember: Sir Brown showed them to us. Ludovic has some, and so do we."

"Yes, but in the note, it is said that *they should find only darkness and sleep in this world*. Darkness and sleep, are the opposite of light and activity."

"So... We can't see them! They're hidden!"

From their room, Caroline and her cousin could hear the parents leaving and the gate closing behind them. The two girls knew they now had the whole house to themselves for a while. Caroline sat on her bed. *Darkness and sleep...* all the messages found were indeed hidden. And what is more, they were all in Caroline's possession. But where are the rest of the things they should find? The teenage girl pulled her hair in anguish.

"Maybe what we are looking for is in this room," she said thoughtfully.

She and Eva looked at each other and said in unison:

"Let's search the room!"

The cousins looked around. Usually, old houses have a lot of secret halls and doors.

"Where do you think we should start?" Eva asked.

"Let's search the floor. There may be open passages."

"The ceramic is not that old. I don't think we'll find anything."

"It doesn't matter. We never know."

With their feet, they felt each pane, each corner. They pushed back a piece of furniture, pulled another. Nothing. Inch by inch, they search. Nothing.

"The ceiling!" said Caroline.

"Did you see its height? It's over 9 feet tall! "

"Let's get the ladder!"

Getting the heavy ladder from the shed up to the first floor was not easy. On several occasions, the teenage girls almost dropped hanging paintings. A few times the ladder scuffed the wall, leaving gray lines on the off-white paint.

Once in their room, the two cousins installed the ladder against the wall where the heraldry had previously been. Eva put down on the floor the bag she was carrying on her shoulder. There was a hammer inside of it. Then she secured the ladder with one foot and with her hands. Caroline climbed it. Using the broomstick, she struck the molding of the ceiling from one point to another. Then she went down, slid the ladder lower and started the maneuver again. Soon, they went around the room. The searches remained vain.

Exhausted, disappointed, they collapsed on their beds. Eva raised her left hand to look at a broken fingernail. Her manicure was ruined.

If you do not get discourage...

The words echoed in Caroline's head. Suddenly, she snapped her fingers.

"We didn't' look in the closet!"

Eva uttered a weary sigh. Her cousin pulled her by the arm, forcing her to get up. Together they completely emptied the closet. The floor was a continuation of the marble tiles of the bedroom and the walls were in mahogany. While one of the girls was to the right, the other went to the left, searching on different corner. Little by little, they came closer and met in the middle.

"There!" cried Caroline. "It sounds hollow!"

"What is it?"

"How would I know?"

Eva handed the hammer to her cousin. Caroline put the back of the hammer into a space between two planks and pulled. The movement caused a good part of a wooden panel to crack. Instinctively, Eva closed her eyes while putting her hands over her ears as if to protect herself from the noise. When she reopened her eyes, her cousin was pulling out a large tube.

Caroline took out an object wrapped in crimson cloth. With infinite precaution, she removed the fabric, and let an old painting unfold.

Chapter 24

he painting depicted a black man standing in a sumptuous setting. He was somewhat going gray and dressed in Regency fashion. He wore a blue coat with red lining and two rows of buttons. From his white trousers hung a key. On his chest was pinned a brooch in the shape of a star. He wore elegantly Hessian boots. His left hand was tucked in one of his pockets. With his right hand in yellow glove, he was leaning on a cane. In that same hand he was holding another glove and a hat, like the those worn by officers in the 19th century. In the background, there was a landscape painting in front of which was installed a table covered with a red cloth. Over the table, a cushion was supporting a royal crown, which was only three-quarters visible. Not too far, a curtain revealed half of a pattern.

"The king's coat of arms!" Caroline exclaimed.

"It's Henry Christophe!" shouted her cousin.

A well-known sound of an engine reached the girls in their bedroom. Eva hurried to check it out through the windows.

"We are in big trouble!" she shouted.

The parents were back and the room was a disaster. The beds, the dressing table, the bedside tables, everything that could move, were grouped in the middle of the room. Clothes were piled up on the beds and other furniture. The bare walls revealed dirty fingerprints. The drawings were piled on the floor, along with the decorative cushions. The stuffed animals were scattered about. And, above all, the doors of the closet were wide open, revealing the piece of torn wood.

Caroline swallowed her saliva.

"This time," she said, "even if they don't listen to us, we have to tell them everything..."

The two teenage girls went down the stairs, one behind the other. Caroline felt pain in her hipbones with every step she took. Inside of her, it was excitement and fear at the same time.

The parents were now in the living room eating some cookies. Caroline slowly walked toward them. She was holding on her arm the painting rolled in the crimson fabric, as one would hold a newborn baby in his blanket.

"Mom, dad, we have something to tell you."

Mr. and Mrs. Lebrun looked at the girls strangely and at the object Caroline was holding. Caroline and Eva gave the impression that the world was ending. Timidly at first, then passionately, Caroline and her cousin recounted the facts that end up to the very minute they discovered the painting.

After listening in silence, Caroline's parents took the painting from her hands and unrolled it again. Scratches made the canvas look like it had holes in it. Her mother delicately placed the crimson fabric on her legs.

"But I know this painting!" exclaimed Mr. Lebrun. "Blain hung it in the living room. And I doubted…"

"Doubted of what?" asked his wife.

"Well, put yourself in my shoes. There is no date, no signature, nothing in this portrait that would really indicate that it's king Henry Christophe circa 1818."

Caroline's father turned to his daughter and niece and gave them a stern look.

"So that was all your *chwichwichwi* (back-and-forth little secretive talks)?!"

"Girls, why didn't you trust us? We have always made you feel comfortable, comfortable enough to tell us anything you wanted. We have never hidden anything from you on anything including this house…This is extremely serious what is happening here. You could have been in some deep trouble."

"We wanted to tell you. But nobody wanted to believe us," replied Caroline.

As they were talking, Caroline and Eva's attention was caught by a piece of paper stuck behind the painting. Gently, Caroline took it off and read it.

"If you have been able to get that far, you will also find the last step that will make you discover the King's treasure."

Caroline jumped out of joy. Her father asked for the paper and he recognized Tonton Blain's handwriting. Mr. Lebrun sat down in astonishment. Beads of sweat covered his forehead. His looked haggard. His mouth was getting dry. This myth he heard so much about, could it be a reality?

"I could have sold the house or had it demolished," he said as if he was talking to himself. "A fire could have reduced the house to ashes along with this treasure which we did not even suspect existed."

"But none of that happened, dad. So, we must find it!"

Mr. Lebrun was lost in serious thought now. Silently, he carefully rolled up the canvas and headed for his study. The others followed him.

"Dad, we have to call Ludovic. We need his help. He's been looking for so long - much longer than us."

"Well..." simply said Mr. Lebrun.

Mr. Lebrun took out a key from his pocket and opened the door of his study. For the rest of the family, the study was like a foreign country that one could only be admitted with some visa and passport. It was the most richly furnished room in the house. The walls were decorated with mahogany wood moldings that rose from the floor to the carved ceiling. Beside Caroline's bedroom, it was the only room whose floor was covered in white marble framed with gold acanthus leaf patterns.

Mr. Lebrun placed the painting on his desk, just below the large chandelier.

"You're right" he replied to his daughter. "But Ludovic is not part of this family. And the way things are going, we don't know what we'll end up finding."

Caroline's father walked around the desk and finally settled down in a large armchair covered in red velvet. Slowly, he ran his fingertips over the bronze encrusted furniture. It was the same metal that adorned the door and the moldings on both the walls and the ceiling.

"Your father is right," added Dr. Lebrun while pulling the heavy velvet curtains that covered the windows.

"Yes, but aunty, it's because of Ludovic's list that we were able to get where we are now."

Mr. Jacques-Victor Henry Lebrun widened his eyes, passed a hand over his head then closes his eyes. Why did François Blain hide the painting? Why did he suggest to his parents to name him Jacques-Victor Henry? Why did he practically give them the house? It was a ridiculous price for such a house. He remembered the conditions…

"Now," said Caroline's mother, "I understand why Blain wanted to do all the repairs himself."

"He didn't want us to find out what he was hiding," retorted Caroline.

"I, I simply don't understand why all these intrigues?" said Mr. Lebrun.

The legend of the *Citadelle*'s treasure was well-known. No one during or after the king's lifetime found it. This treasure fed the imagination of many from Sir Brown down to the three teenagers and probably beyond if they do not find it. Have François-Ferdinand Blain cracked the mystery? How could he say that it existed and, even better, that he had it?

Chapter 25

aroline and her cousin were the first to get out of beds the next morning. In fact, no one really slept at the Lebruns the night before. Caroline's father spent most of it doing research in his study. Her mother, meanwhile, turned all the notes she thought relevant into a list. Caroline and Eva fed this list with their thoughts and the many details they remembered during their research.

When the parents came downstairs that morning, Caroline and Eva were speculating in the kitchen while munching on some oranges. Mr. Lebrun went straight to the coffeepot and poured himself a cup which he sweetened more than usual.

"Caroline, call Ludovic and ask him to come here later this afternoon."

Caroline jumped on her father's neck and covered his face with kisses. It was exactly what she wanted. She and Eva could not imagine continuing their search without him.

"Ok, ok...," said Mr. Lebrun with a half-smile. "But don't tell him more."

"Alright dad!"

"I hope I will be able to come back home early," said Dr. Lebrun.

"Do you really have to go, mom?"

"I can't work from home like your father. I have to see a lot of patients today at the clinic. I'll try to come back as soon as I can. But it's not guaranteed."

"Don't worry, honey. We'll be waiting for you. In fact, last night I spoke with Charles. He will come here. After talking to him, I will know what to do."

Caroline smiled. Finally, she was going to talk to this man without feeling like she was chasing after him. His father could read the excitement in her eyes. Indeed, at the announcement of the arrival of the expert, Eva and her could no longer stay calm. Mr. Lebrun was afraid that in this frenzy, the two girls would share something his friend should by no means know.

After the departure of his wife, Mr. Lebrun was barely finishing giving some instructions to the girls on what to do, when the auctioneer arrived with a bag under his arms.

"My friend, yesterday, you called me just at the right time," said Charles as he took a seat in one of the red armchairs in the study. "I was preparing to go straight to the law firm this morning. Here's the report you wanted."

"Oh, great! Thank you. It's the piece of evidence that was missing... Do you have some time for some coffee?"

"Sure. I never say no to coffee."

Mr. Lebrun came out of his study and asked the girls to help him bring the coffee. This was the signal that Caroline and her cousin were waiting for. On a tray, they quickly set a coffee pot, a sugar bowl, and two cups and brought it to the study.

"Hello Mr. Philippe."

"Good God, Caroline! How have you grown! The last time I saw you, you were no bigger than two tangerines."

Caroline smiled because it had not been that long since she last saw him. She was amused at the countless times her childish size was compared to a tropical fruit. Her father took the opportunity to introduce his niece.

"To have such pretty young girls at home! You are blessed!"

"Thank you, my friend... Would you like some milk with the coffee?"

"No thank you... I like my coffee plain."

"Me too..."

Mr. Lebrun paused, then resumed with a serious look in his face.

"I have two paintings that I would like you to see."

Caroline and Eva remained standing, silent. Mr. Charles Philippe looked at his watch around his somewhat chubby wrist.

"No problem. You know how much I admire the decor of this house. It reminds me so much of our dear Blain. The Law and the art world as well have lost an outstanding gentleman," added the auctioneer with sadness.

"Yes, indeed," replied Mr. Lebrun. "Mr. Blain was a great man."

While keeping the painting rolled, Caroline took the portrait of the three women and hand it to her father.

"Hmmm.... It's a beautiful piece. Did you just buy it? Because when I last authenticated the coins and the little landscape painting, I don't remember seeing this."

"It's been in the family for years. I always wanted to have it appraised, but it completely escaped my mind."

"Well, you have a remarkable work there! But do you have a certificate? Any paperwork?"

Caroline thought about the letters.

"No," her father replied. "Maybe my grandparents had a certificate. I don't know…"

"It's ok. This often happens in the case of old works that people inherit… The touch is very similar to that of certain Italian masters of the mid-1800's. The 1840 date confirms it. Do you know who the characters are in the painting?"

"Queen Marie-Louise Christophe and her daughters," said Mr. Lebrun.

"The Queen and her daughters? Are you sure?"

"Certain."

"You have to cherish a great deal," urged the auctioneer. "Very few portraits of the queen or her daughters exist."

Mr. Charles Philippe crossed his arms over his chest, just above his big belly and breathed deeply while looking at the canvas.

"You know, the last time I saw a painting of one of the Queen's daughters was at the home of an old gentleman in Cape-Haitian who collects everything related to the kingdom of Henri Christophe."

Caroline and her cousin's eyes widened. A smile formed on their lips. Caroline came forward.

"Was it Sir Bown?" she asked urgently.

"Sir Brown! That's it!" cried Mr. Charles Philippe, clapping one hand against the other. "You know him?"

"Yes," replied the two cousins in unison.

"We met him in Cap-Haitian during a trip with our school," said Caroline.

"He had the portrait of *Madame Première* in his living room," informed Eva.

"That's right! A very beautiful painting! In my life, I think I have seen only four portraits of the Queen's daughters, the one that belongs to you being the fourth. Besides, it's precisely this man... what was his name again?"

"Sir Brown..."

"Yes. It's thanks to Sir Brown that the MUPANAH is aware of the existence of a painting of the children of the king. Maybe one day we can repatriate it."

Caroline remembered that painting. Sir Brown described it to them. In it, Prince Jacques Henri is dressed in Regency fashion and behind him, his sisters wore white muslin garbs, gloved, with high hairdo and a row of pearls.

Mr. Lebrun left his chair and reached for the rolled painting representing Henry Christophe. Gently, he unrolled it under the seasoned eyes of his friend.

"That's another work. Although I know who it is, we've never been able to go back to the precise date of its creation."

Mr. Charles Philippe took a magnifying glass out of his bag and scanned the painting over its entire surface.

"Wonderful!"

"Mr. Blain gave it to us before his death. He too was trying to date it."

"Blain was a great collector," said the auctioneer. "This painting is an extraordinary copy!"

"A copy?" Caroline wondered.

"Probably yes. You know, in 1816, Richard Evans painted an original and two copies. One is in the *Musée du Panthéon National* in Champs de Mars…"

"At the MUPANAH museum?" blurted out Eva.

Like her cousin, Caroline too was surprised. In elementary levels, her school, like many schools in the capital, organized visits to this museum. But she did not remember having seen this portrait there.

"Yes. At the MUPANAH," said the auctioneer. "One of the portraits was sent as a gift to England to William

Wilberforce. Christophe ordered it from Richard Evans to thank him for his precious help."

"Who was this person?" Caroline asked.

"Wilberforce was an English abolitionist. He and Thomas Clarkson worked for the abolition of slavery and the advancement of blacks. The two men collaborated with Christophe to help him establish his kingdom but also to prove to the rest of the world that blacks were not idiots."

Caroline thought about what her teacher had told her about the family that helped the queen in Europe.

"Were the two men Christophe's friends?" she asked.

"Absolutely. It was also with the Clarksons that the queen, the princesses, and their servants stayed for some time when they arrived in England."

"But, Mr. Philippe," intervened Eva, "you said that Richard Evans painted an original and two copies. If we have a copy, the MUPANAH has another, where is the third one?"

"In fact, the MUPANAH one is the second one. Christophe had it made for Tsar Alexandre 1st of Russia."

Mr. Lebrun shook his head. He was confused.

"I'm not following you," he said.

"It seems that Christophe admired this sovereign for his position against slavery and the slave trade. This painting was a present from him and it's this copy that is at the MUPANAH."

"How did we get it back?" asked Mr. Lebrun.

"In London, at an auction, at Christies."

Caroline remembered the fan that Sir Brown also bought at an auction. She wondered if Mr. Philippe had seen it...

"Then," she asked with a beating heart, "who has the original?"

"That's the real dilemma. It's is unclear which of Wilberforce or the Tsar received the original. But one thing for sure, this one is a copy of the very hands of Richard Evans."

"But why paint the same portrait several times?" Eva asked.

"Well, we are not in the times of photocopiers. You must remember that Evans was a famous copyist of his time. He alone was therefore able to reproduce his work so faithfully if the king wanted several copies to offer as gifts."

Mr. Charles Philippe, while finishing his cup of coffee, looked at the two cousins.

"Remember this, girls: our history is even richer than what the books want us to believe. I encourage you to delve into the full extent of our great culture!"

"Indeed," said Caroline's father pensively. "Haitian art is rich."

"Very rich in history… Alright, friends! I must go. I have a lot to do this morning. If you need anything Mr. Lebrun, you know where to find me. Thank you for the good cup of coffee, girls!"

Chapter 26

an you imagine, Dad! Our painting has as much value as the one in MUPANAH!" said Caroline.

"Yes. That's great... I wonder now which path should we follow?" Mr Lebrun asked.

"Uncle, there must be something Tonton Blain said or did while he was alive that only you know. Maybe you could think about that."

"And we," continued Caroline, "we are going to try to see if there is anything else in the room that we could discover."

Caroline's father stared at the two teenage girls who were speaking with forceful gestures. They were brimming with an energy he had never seen before.

"Please.... Please... Whatever you both discover, do not tear down the house. Call me first. Do you both understand?"

"Yes, sir! Yes, sir!" said both girls.

They ran back upstairs. The mess of the day before was still there.

"We should rearrange the room," suggested Eva.

"But while we're doing that, I think we should check out the spots we haven't searched yet."

"Good idea!"

But as the hours passed, neither the girls or Mr. Lebrun found something. Caroline did not want to give up. It was because of their persistence that they made new discoveries.

Caroline's mother came back as soon as she could. Without giving her time to put down her bag, the two teenage girls start to tell her in detail what the auctioneer revealed to them. While taking off her shoes, Mrs. Lebrun listened attentively.

"Girls," she said after a while, "what made you both go and search your room?"

Caroline thought for a moment.

"It was because dad said that the heraldry was in there."

"And then," added Eva, "it's also there that we discovered the first note."

"Honey, when you visited Blain when he was alive, do you remember seeing the same thing somewhere else in the house?"

All heads turned to Mr. Lebrun. Caroline crossed her arms and stared at her father. She looked like she was about to leap in the direction he would point.

Mr. Lebrun reflected for a moment. Mentally he walked through every room of the house. He never noticed seeing this drawing anywhere but in Caroline's bedroom.

"Wait!" said his wife. "Do you remember how you disapproved of Blain keeping on fixing up the house when he already sold it to us?"

"Yes…"

"And how he was having fun doing so especially with Caroline's room and your study?"

"Keep going…"

"Look at the bookcase against the wall in your study. You told me once there were only two bookcases, not just one covering so much wall space."

"Right… There was a large leather sofa between the two. And above the sofa, on the wall…."

Mr. Lebrun looked at his wife, hid daughter, and his niece.

"On the wall, the heraldry of the Simons!" he finally said in a breath.

"The Simons?!" repeated Caroline and her cousin in a cry.

"Yes."

"Dad, Louis-Achille Simon was the king's right-hand man! He knew everything about the royal family!"

"So, he knew where the treasure was!" added Eva.

"Lord, have mercy!" blurted out Caroline's mother.

All four of them walked towards and stares at the bookcase. Mr. Lebrun cleared the top of his desk and then rolled up his sleeves.

"Put all the books from the library on top of the desk!" he ordered.

In a moment, the shelves of the bookcase were emptied. Caroline went with her cousin to get the ladder and a hammer. It was the right instrument. Under the watchful eyes of his family, Mr. Lebrun meticulously dismantled the customed-made bookcase.

Caroline was getting impatient. Her father was going too slowly for her liking. She wanted to take the hammer from him and smash the wood panels.

But her father was in no hurry. He wanted to make sure he would not destroy any evidence that will help them solve the puzzle.

"Wow!" said everyone when they finally saw the wall.

In the middle of it, there was indeed a hidden heraldry. A fine cedar carving of a coat of arms was hanging proudly and looking as if it had been made the day before. Caroline was in complete shock.

"Why did Tonton Blain have the Espérances and the Simons heraldry in his house?" she asked after a while.

"I don't know," replied her father. "He only told me that it had been in this family for generations."

"Then, the Espérances and the Simons are not only related to Ludovic but also to his uncle?" asked Dr. Lebrun.

"It's possible," replied her husband. "After all, there were half-brothers on their paternal side. Perhaps this is where they share their ancestry."

Caroline was biting her lips. Her eyes were fixed on the heraldry.

"What's the matter?" Eva asked.

"Ludovic. Won't we wait for him?" she asked.

Everyone indeed forgot the young man. The two cousins already called him and told him when he was supposed to come. Mr. Lebrun took his cell phone out of his pocket and handed it to his daughter.

"Call him. He should have been here already."

Caroline called, but no one answered. Almost at the same time, the maid knocked on the study's door to let it be known that a young man has arrived.

Ludovic was surprised to find Caroline and her whole family locked in the study. It was the first time he had set foot in it. The rich décor intimidated him. He looked around. Books were lying everywhere. Pieces of wood were piled up on the floor. A silent stare from the Lebruns greeted him.

"We need to talk to you," said Mr. Lebrun.

Ludovic gaped at the heraldry on the wall. He got closer while listening to the story. He could not believe what he was hearing. But, above all, he wondered how his grandfather was able to keep such a great secret during all these years. But Caroline's father knew François-Ferdinand Blain. He knew that he was not a man to do things half way.

"There must be more to all this," he said thoughtfully.

"Let's dismantle the other two parts of the bookcase, Dad!"

"Let's do it!"

The other two parts were higher than the middle one. Ludovic offered to take apart the furniture. From the bottom of the ladder, Caroline and her cousin were sweating profusely. The girls collected each piece that Ludovic removed and piled it on the floor. For her part, Caroline's mother was stacking the books in a corner of the study.

Time to time, without coming down the ladder, Ludovic pressed his face to the wall to look behind the remaining shelves.

"What do you see? asked Mr. Lebrun.

"It looks like… a door!"

Ludovic doubled in speed and ardor. Soon, an antique mahogany door appeared. It was carved and framed in bronze. It had the same patterns as the desk. On the lintel of the door, Caroline recognized something to be another heraldry.

"The Queen's coat of arms," she said softly.

Ludovic's heart was racing. He could not believe his eyes. The molding of the doorjamb was the same as that of his mirror.

Mr. Lebrun stared at the door. He was both fascinated and frightened. Then he took a deep breath, put his hand on the handle and opened it.

"Is there a light switch, Dad?"

An anxious feeling gripped Caroline, making her stomach ache. The opening angle of the door did not allow light from the study to enter the small room. Mr. Lebrun teetered and finally found a switch. A dim light then shoots out from the cobwebs. Everyone rushed to the entrance of the room. Caroline entered first.

"Ooooh!" she cried out. "So many! So many!"

"*All these objects fashioned with such artful hand!*" screamed Eva.

"*Which must find darkness and sleep in this world!*" shouted Ludovic.

Chapter 27

The room was exploding with precious items. The group entered cautiously. They were witnessing a true treasure trove of objects: tapestries, paintings, chairs, tables, clocks, porcelain, silverware – they were all stamped with heraldry from the reign of Henry Christophe.

"Wow!" said Caroline. "Look Ludovic! Your mirror! There are many here!"

The young man noticed the two large mirrors identical to the one his grandfather gave him. A chain of hands was formed to take out the objects one after the other.

While Caroline was completely overwhelmed with joy, she observed a certain uneasiness with Ludovic. He was sweating profusely and his hands were shaking. A full harness with its golden spurs almost slipped from his hand. *Sans-Souci* and *Citadelle* blue prints crumpled a little under his fingers.

"Are you alright?" asked Caroline.

"Uh… yeah," Ludovic replied timidly.

"What is that?" asked Mr. Lebrun.

All attention turned on him. He was facing a chest in front of a mahogany chair which armrests were carved as a woman's busts. The front legs were golden bronze lion paws.

Helped by Ludovic and the two teenage girls, Mr. Lebrun took the safe out of the room. The lock was already forced. The safe was just waiting to be opened. No one dared to speak. All were waiting.

Finally, Mr. Lebrun opened. In the first compartment, there was a large navy-blue velvet box. It held an envelope and on it there was the subscription:

To

Jacques-Victor Henry Lebrun

Mr. Lebrun looked at his wife than the children. He gathered all his strength. He opened the envelope and read out loud the content.

"Dearest Jacques,

Today I am even more proud of you than I have ever been since you came into this world. If you are reading this letter, it is because you have been able to discover the royal treasure.

Congratulations!

What will follow is my story. I could not tell you this earlier because you would not have believed me. But I trust Caroline. She is as stubborn and reckless as I was at her age. So, take your time to read this. Because you will not find anyone who can help you.

Claire Henry, my maternal grandmother, was one of the children that Henry Christophe had before his marriage. Although they were almost the same age, Madame Christophe befriended her and took her under her wings.

Marie-Louise Christophe made sure that she received the best education. When the monarchy was established, she became one of the ladies of honor at the Palais Sans-Souci. She was known as Claire Twist.

The Earl of Citronade, whose real name was Louis-Achille Simon, was Christophe's most trusted friend. He was one of his few allies. Soon he and Claire fell in love. Preparations for the wedding went well. Everything was planned for the end of the year 1821.

But unforeseen events decided otherwise. A revolt broke out. The king committed suicide. The royal family was dissolved. But Claire remained faithful to the queen and her daughters.

To save the royal treasures, the earl pretended to ally himself with those who plundered the Citadelle Laferrière. He knew the exact location of the treasure, for on several occasions he had helped the king to bury his personal fortune there.

Sometime later, the earl visited his fiancée in the house where Christophe's wife and daughters were kept safe. He informed Queen Marie-Louise of his plans and renewed his complete devotion to her. Then, he begged her to accept the protection offered by President Boyer to go to

Port-au-Prince and to bring Claire with her. The queen was quick to follow his advice.

For several months, the earl devoted himself to recovering what he could from Cap-Henry and securing everything. Including one of the three copies of the portrait of Henry Christophe painted by Richard Evans. As soon as everything was in order, he headed for the capital.

Traumatized by the scenes of lootings at Sans-Souci, the queen refused to let the earl give her the king's gold coins or other objects he had been able to save. She begged him to keep them safe until she could find a way to get hold of them.

The right moment never came. Unfortunately, the queen left for England with her daughters. Louis-Achille Simon married Claire on August 12, 1821, the day after the queen's departure.

The Simons not once had the ambition to make this treasure theirs. During the queen's exile, they waited indefinitely for her return. They regained hope when they learned that Madame Christophe wanted to return to the country as a citizen and not as a queen. However, permission would be granted too late to her.

The idea of starting a list came to mind when my ancestors learned of her death a few years later. Christophe and his family decimated; Claire Henry Simon became heiress. Inspired by the frequent correspondence she had with Queen Marie-Louise, Claire wrote two acrostics that would allow the children of future generations to never tire of taking care of their heritage.

While I was able to keep these acrostics, the genealogical list got lost. And I am still trying to find out who could have taken it away from me – although it does not matter. It contained the following information…

Caroline and Eva immediately recognized Ludovic's list; a real dynasty inspired by Henry Christophe. His great-uncle took the time to mention each date and describe the king's coat of arms in great details as well as each family heraldry. He also spoke of various objects that the descendants of the Simons were able to recover over the years and all those that they bequeathed to MUPANAH.

... My mother, Ann-Athénaïre Blain, was born a Démaille. It's after her death that my father married the mother of my half-brother, Xavier Paul. This man made me suffer so much that I will not speak of him here.

Rather, I want to celebrate the happiness you and your family have given me. Your late father was for me the brother that nature could not give me. And you, the son whom my health has refused me.

This is my story which today becomes yours. From now on, Caroline and you are the protectors of this treasure. I am leaving, confident that you, my beloved son, will know how to defend it tirelessly."

François-Ferdinand Henry Blain

Chapter 28

It was in absolute silence that Mr. Lebrun slowly placed the letter on his desk. Thus, it was not the queen who started Ludovic's list but a daughter of the Earl of Citronade. It was her who had this fine, slender, and nervous handwriting.

Caroline felt embarrassed. She looked at Ludovic out of the corner of her eye. He stood disappointed about lineage. The Espérances, the Simons, and the Twists blood were not in his family tree. Caroline moved closer to him, put her arm around his neck, and rested her head on his shoulder. Caroline, Eva, and her parents understood the sadness of the young man.

Mr. Lebrun retuned to the chest and opened the velvet box. In it, a golden necklace from which hung a star. The star was a hexagram with double blue points. Between them six other small gold points connected in the center by a medallion. The links of the necklace were double knotted and regularly separated by medals representing a crowned phoenix. These words were engraved in French on the bordering frame: *Prix de la Valeur* – Price of Valor.

Mr. Lebrun handed the box to Caroline. Her heart was pounding so hard it felt like it was coming out of her mouth.

"There's another envelope and a message," noticed her father.

> *"If he stands next to you,*
> *then he too is an heir of this cause.*
> *Give him his letter.*
> *But if he is not here, burn it. "*
>
> F-F. B.

"It's for you Ludovic," said Mr. Lebrun.

"For me?" wondered the young man.

Ludovic looked at Caroline. The teenage girl gave him an encouraging smile. But he was nailed by emotion. Caroline took the letter and put it in his hands.

The color of Ludovic's envelope was lighter than that of Mr. Lebrun's letter. It seemed to have been placed in the chest just before the lawyer's death. Feverishly Ludovic read it. His voice faded. His hands trembled. As he went on, he smiled more and more and mumbled often.

In the letter, François-Ferdinand Blain revealed how much he regretted to have never had the opportunity to share anything with him. He told him how he kept up with the news of the young man since birth through his mother; how he wished things were different between him and his grandfather; how he hoped his mother would eventually agree to put him in Audubon School knowing all the support that he would receive from the principal. He also told him that if he was reading this letter, it was because, as he wished, he had become closer to the Lebruns; and from henceforth, just as he himself had done all his life, he was sure that he also was going to defend the cause.

Caroline could not believe that Tonton Blain knew Ludovic's mother and that she never said anything about it. Nobody could believe how the old man found a clever a way to force the two children to meet by placing them in the same school and classroom.

Ludovic took a deep long breath and tears ran down his cheeks. He could not contain himself.

Caroline did not know how to console him. It was not the reaction she expected. She taught that after all these months of fruitless research, Ludovic would have celebrated.

"Listen to me Ludo," said Dr. Lebrun in her soft and authoritarian voice. "What happened between your uncle and your grandfather has no importance. This treasure could have been squandered over the years and no one would have ever known about it. On the contrary, you should be proud to have been chosen to help carry out this intrigue."

"Mom is right," said Caroline. "You, Eva, and I are heirs to this cause."

"Don't worry Ludovic. My wife and I will talk to your mother tomorrow night... Now, all of you come! We must see what more is hidden at the bottom of this chest!"

Carefully, Mr. Lebrun lifted the second velvet cover on top of which Ludovic's letter was placed.

"Oh!!!" yelled out Caroline.

Sparkling jewels were at the bottom of the chest. Earrings, necklaces, bracelets, rings in diamonds, sapphires, emeralds, amethysts, rubies shined. Unimaginable precious stones. Stacked separately next to the jewels were several tiaras of all colors.

Caroline pulled out a tiara and placed it on her head. The translucent yellow of the stone shone. She grabbed a necklace and laid it on her palm. Never in her life has she seen such wonders. Eva took an emerald pendant and tried it on. There were so many jewels that Caroline's mother decided to get on the act too. She took some out of the chest. The top of the desk was soon filled with blue, red, green ones. The kaleidoscopic stones blinded them.

Mr. Lebrun suddenly sank back into his chair. He casted a vague gaze on his daughter, his niece, and his wife. They were trying on jewelry after jewelry. On the other hand, Ludovic was interested in utensils stamped with the coat of arms of the queen.

Caroline finally looked up and saw that her father was unphased by the excitement around him. All the weight of the world seemed to fall on his back.

"Are you ok?" asked his wife who also noticed his weariness.

Caroline's father raised his hands to the sky and then let them fall on his sides.

"I'm just a citizen. I'm just a man like any other and now, in a few hours, I became the heir of a royal treasure."

This treasure, which has been a legend for almost two centuries, was in their house. A big chunk of that treasure was laying in front of Mr. Lebrun, challenging his skills as a lawyer. The objects were lying in the middle of the room.

A century old treasure.

An unexpected legacy.

Mr. Lebrun closed his eyes while gently rubbing his forehead. He was pondering about the best thing to do.

"I think we all need to sleep on it," he finally said while getting up.

However, the next day, when she met her father in his study, Caroline saw that he had not slept. His eyes were puffy. He did not shave. He obviously thought deeply about the best decision to make.

Eva was followed by Ludovic when she joined them. Dr. Lebrun locked the door of the study. All eyes were on the envelope that Ludovic had in his hand.

"It's the original," he said.

"Can we see it?" asked Dr. Lebrun.

Carefully, Ludovic put the envelope with his list on the desk. The yellowed, torn, gnawed paper was kept inside a small plastic bag. Cut in two, it was as if it could disintegrate at any moment.

"Fantastic!" exclaimed Caroline.

Eva and Caroline were excited to see the list. But they had something to show to Ludovic too.

"King Henry 1st," proudly said Caroline.

Ludovic looked at the painting. He remembered seeing it in books during his research. But having the original in front of him was breathtaking.

Mr. Lebrun put down the family tree, then cleared his throat.

"We wanted to let you know, after much consideration, that the portrait of Henry Christophe will remain in the family."

Shouts of joy greeted the news. Caroline and her cousin clapped with all their might.

"Girls, let me finish... Caroline, you, your mother, and Eva can choose some jewelry that you would like to have. Ludovic, you can also take one for your mother."

"Thank you, Mr. Lebrun," said the happy young man.

"You're welcome... Everything we will choose for ourselves will be our heritance, our private collection."

"And what will we do with the rest?" asked Eva.

"We will share it with the Haitian government."

"Why?" Caroline protested.

"Listen up children, we will never be able to wear all these jewels and even less parade ourselves around town with all these precious stones. On the other hand, what a testimony to our cultural heritage and history! They need to be displayed somewhere, a museum for future generations."

Caroline jumped out of joy.

"You are right dad! What better way for us all to defended the cause!"

Epilogue

he devastating earthquake that hit Port-au-Prince in January 12, 2010 did not destroy the *Musée du Panthéon Nationale* (National Museum) located in *Champ de Mars*.

In 2018, during a live auction held in New York by the *Alexander Art Gallery*, the Haitian Government acquired the painting entitled *"Les Enfants du Roi Henry Christophe"* (The Children of King Henry Christophe). Since October 6, 2020, that painting became officially part of the historical and cultural heritage of Haiti.

As for Queen Marie-Louise Coidavid Christophe, her name is immortalized in Great-Britain by one of the over nine hundred Blue Plaques in that country. Hers was affixed on February 7, 2022 on the walls of the 49 Weymouth Street located in the Marylebone district where she and her daughters lived from 1821 to 1824.

About the Author

Pascale Doxy is a native of Haiti. There she worked for over a decade in the school system. After immigrating to the US, she embraced her interest in painting, and her success has been recognized by the American media, including various magazines.

Pascale is also a passionate writer, and her art often mirrors the texts she writes. She is the author of the bilingual poetry collection *Journal d'Étrangers / Foreign Diary* and also of *Concerto of the Heart*, a poetry collection published in both French and English.

Heirs to a Cause is her first novel.